D0761787

THE WEDDING CONTRACT

A FERRO FAMILY NOVEL

H.M. Ward

www.SexyAwesomeBooks.com

H.M. Ward Press

COPYRIGHT

H.M. Ward Press
First Edition: May 2014
ISBN: 978-1630350185

FOREWORD
By
Michael Ward

Weddings are rife with stories. Before Holly became H.M. Ward, author extraordinaire, the two of us owned a photography studio that focused on weddings. And, somehow, that led to our buying a bridal shop at some point. (It made perfect sense at the time.) For years, we lived and breathed weddings.

Weddings are crazy – and the crazy is contagious. But, the stories! The stories almost make it all worthwhile. Sometimes they're sweet. There were the high school sweethearts that drifted apart, made some wrong turns, and battled through the years, only to rediscover each other in their golden years and tie the knot with their grandkids in the wedding party. And then there were the laughable, crazy stories that no one would believe if they hadn't revolved around a wedding.

I've never had anyone doubt a crazy wedding story, because everyone knows that anything is possible at a wedding. When you take two families that are practically strangers to one another, put them together for a day that revolves around the childhood dreams of a girl, the hopes every parent has for their children, and a bill that looks like it could be a mortgage, people can get kinda nuts. And that kind of nuttiness makes for great stories – writing one that's entirely fiction would almost seem like cheating.

So, as you read The Wedding Contract, know that Holly did her research on this one! I always see a little bit of Holly and me in her stories. Avery's "spray-start" car? I took Holly out on a lot of dates in that car (I know, I really knew how to woo a girl.) But, The Wedding Contract?

The boob-flashing bridesmaid never paid me any attention... Holly had all the luck.

THE WEDDING CONTRACT

CHAPTER 1

I can hear Amy's voice through the front wall of the little shop, talking to a potential client about photography for their wedding. I'm in the back, putting away props from this morning's shoot. After stowing the box on a shelf in the back, I walk across the open space, and duck out through the curtain that covers the doorway to the front.

"Well, congratulations, and thank you for considering Bella Chicks Studio. Best of luck to you both." Amy smiles as she sets the phone back into the cradle. Her light brown hair is pin straight and tied back into a style that looks perfect on her. When I try it, my curls just look tangled.

Folding my arms over my chest, I breathe in slowly. It's stupid to think that this was his doing. Amy hasn't even told me yet, but the skin on my arms prickles like a big fat omen. I know it was him. It's always him. "So, I take it the Gettys hired someone else?"

Amy smiles at me. It's the facial expression that begs, 'Don't kill the messenger!' I'm not mad at Amy; I'm upset about the situation. We can't keep losing clients like this. She nods slowly. "Yeah, they went with Bella Clicks."

My lips smash together and I try not to yell. I try so hard not to overreact, but this is the third client that Nick Ferro has stolen from me this month. The bastard has been making my eye twitch for weeks. It seems like every time I figure out how to get a step ahead of him, he one-ups me, and then does it better and cheaper. God, I hate him.

The worst part is, if things continue like this, I can't afford to stay in my little shop. Babylon Village is cute, but the rent is a bitch. And I know Mr. Copycat doesn't have that issue because his daddy owns the damn shopping center. Why didn't I get a non-compete clause in my lease contract?

Amy can tell that my blood is boiling. "Uh, Sky. You haven't blinked in like, five minutes. Don't go all Medusa on me." Amy is a mythology buff and works Greek gods into anything and everything. Half the time I don't even know what she's talking about.

The ringing in my ears should be my cue to go scream in the back room like a normal small business owner. Instead, I knot my tightly folded arms and shove through the glass front door. My feet pound the parking lot, hard and fast, leaving Amy and her don't-do-its behind.

This has to stop. I was doing fine until Nick showed up. God knows there are enough people trying to make a living in New York, but none of them, aside from this ass-hat, camped out on my doorstep stealing my clients.

I never do stuff like this. I never chew anyone out. I always smile and look for the bright side of things. Screw that. I'll be out of business if I don't fight back, so I shove into his store, my fists up and fangs bared.

"Get out of here, you sorry excuse for a man!" I'm standing in his perfect lobby, which is just as posh as mine, but instead of rich red accents, his are blue. He has his consultation table in the same spot as mine, with huge pictures of brides in Time Square and by Saint Pat's Cathedral, just like I do. I notice the new floral arrangements with peacock feathers, and I'm ready to explode. When did he copy those?

My eyes drift over to the little table he has set up with albums on it. Last month, I met a new vendor that provides these beautiful albums for my boudoir clients. The albums have sequins, supple leather, and feel perfect under your fingertips. I see one glinting from behind a wedding album on his table. Wide-eyed, I step toward it and lift the little book with shaking hands.

Nick appears from the back and shakes his head slowly. "Sky Thompson, what can I do for you?" Nick has dark, perfectly tousled hair that falls over his forehead, right above gem-colored blue eyes. Today, he's wearing a designer white button-down shirt with jeans. There's a chunky watch on his wrist that cost more than my net worth. He's beautiful, cocky, and rich. His voice is like a siren's song, and he completely and totally sucks rabid monkeys—a spoiled brat to the core.

Anger surges through me, as I look up at him. "What'd you do to land the Getty wedding? Offer to pose with her in the boudoir pictures?" Oh my god. Nick has the audacity to smile while I'm ranting. He tries to hide it, but I can see the amusement in his eyes. I shove a finger into his chest and continue raving. "Because there's no way you could get that client on your own, you pampered ass!"

Nick looks like he's biting the inside of his mouth to keep from laughing. I'm right in front of him and seriously consider kicking his shins. Every muscle in my body is strung so tight that I'm ready to explode. I'm practically vibrating—until I see Beverly Getty emerge from the back room, followed by her daughter and husband. Awh, suck.

I deflate as I see the livid look on Beverly's face. She told me that she'd be sending a check today, but she's in Nick's studio instead. I don't get it, and from the look on her face, she doesn't plan to elaborate. "What did you say about my daughter? Or was your crass comment directed at me, Miss Thompson?"

What the fuckery? Seriously, I never blow off steam! I never tell anyone that they suck and the one time I do, it bites me on the ass. My lips tug into a nervous smile and I have that weird feeling where I don't know what to do with my hands. I grab my pointer finger and try to patch things up, like I didn't just eat my foot. No, I swallowed my whole damn leg and half my ass. There's no way to make this right. "Mrs. Getty, I didn't mean to imply—"

"You didn't imply anything, dear. And if you must know, we found Nick to be much more easygoing. A wedding is stressful enough and I didn't want anything else to make my Tiffany anxious. I see I chose well and I'll make sure that everyone knows how you really behave."

Nick glances between us before putting a hand on Beverly's shoulder. "Sky wouldn't have ruined your daughter's wedding. She's a very capable photographer. The truth is, she only gets twitchy like this when she forgets her meds. It could happen to anyone." Beverly Getty gives me a second look, like she can now see my obvious mental defect.

"Go back and grab a chai tea from the Keurig. I'll get those new albums I mentioned." He looks up at me and grins. "On your way, Sky. Or would you prefer I call Amy to fetch you?" He says it so sweetly, as if he's helping me.

Not meaning to, I clutch my hands tightly and growl before I turn on my heel and storm out. As the door closes behind me, I hear Nick saying to the Gettys, "Don't worry, she's not dangerous."

CHAPTER 2

Amy is standing in the doorway when I get back. My eyes are stinging and I want to cry. I go straight into the back and she trails behind me like a faithful puppy. "Sky, what happened? It can't be that bad!"

"I called Tiffany Getty a slut and suggested that the only reason they signed with Nick was to touch his naked chest!" I'm sniffling hard, trying not to cry—not before I find the tissue box. I head over to the prop shelves and start digging around. A crate of plastic apples topples off the shelf, onto the floor, spilling apples in every direction.

"Well, that's not that bad." She has a quizzical tone to her voice that tells me she doesn't understand.

"The Gettys were there! All three of them walked out from the back of his shop. Her dad looked like he wanted to slit my throat and toss me into the canal."

Amy averts her eyes. "Oh, well, yeah. That's kinda bad."

I find the little tissue box and sink to the floor. "That's not the worst part. Nick told them that I'm usually fine—that I only get like this when I forget my meds. So I went from being a bitch to being crazy!" Holding the tissue over my face, I take a deep breath. I need to calm down, but I can't.

"Oh, honey. It's okay. It's all going to be okay." She kneels next to me and rubs my shoulder.

"How can you say that? He's ruined me. My business is falling apart because of him. The guy is a parasite and you're telling me that it's all okay?" I'm not usually like this. I don't fall to pieces over little things, but it's so far past little that I can't take it anymore. I went from having a thriving shop to sneak-sleeping in the store. I have no apartment, no money, and thanks to Nick, I lost the Getty wedding.

"Of course it's okay. Everyone knew you were crazy already." She smiles and leans in, giving me a hug.

"Gee, thanks."

"Seriously, Sky. Cut yourself some slack. You won't close with every client. Some of them will choose someone else. You can't beat yourself up when one gets away." She only says that because she doesn't know how bad it is. I've been hiding it from her. Amy has enough stuff to worry about, I haven't wanted to add more to her pile.

But it's going to become very obvious, very soon. I clutch my face and don't look up. My gaze is fixated on the floor. "Go look at the calendar. My close-rate got cut in half after the ass-hat moved in. Clients walk out of here with my packet in hand, and I swear to God that he looks it over, offers them the same coverage for less money, and then gives them an extra album. I don't even have a chance."

Amy continues to encourage me. "Sky, you're better than him. You're the one who comes up with the newest ideas."

"But, Amy, a week later, he has them, too!"

"Do you remember that Trash-the-Dress session in the city? It was so much fun. And you have another client thinking about booking a similar session. Don't let him get you down. There will always be people trying to get a piece of what you have, Sky, because you're the best. They want to be you."

Her words calm me down enough to look up. She smiles and hands me one of the fancy mirrors we use in pin-up shoots. "It looks like a dog licked your face."

My mascara is running down my cheeks and a big smear of eye shadow looks like dirt on my temple. The corner of my mouth twitches.

"Sky," Amy begins, "you have a new idea, don't you?"

"Yeah." I stare into the glass, my imagination running wild. The picture hasn't fully formed in my mind yet, but I can see the client in the water, make-up darkened and smeared. Something unusual and tragic. It's like nothing I've ever shot before and very un-bride-like, but amazing all the same.

Amy waves a hand in front of my face to catch my attention. "Hello? Are you going to try it this weekend with Sophie?"

"If she lets me." My eyes flick up over the top of the mirror. "It would be so cool, and Shelter Island is the perfect place to do it." I bite my bottom lip, thinking about the logistics, and hand the mirror back to Amy to be put away.

"I wish I was coming with you. Five days out there sounds awesome—especially at this time of year. I bet it's beautiful." Amy stands and brushes herself off. She usually comes with me to carry gear and help out, but this wedding is small and I'm doing it at cost as a favor to a childhood friend. The only money I'll make is from print sales after the wedding.

I say her new name out loud. "Sophie Stevens. I can't believe she's getting married."

"Yeah, but Stevens is a lot easier to say, am I right?"

"Yeah, Poloiscitiano doesn't exactly roll off the tongue."

Amy resumes her duties at the front desk, preparing paperwork. "Go home, Sky. Pack and take an earlier ferry out. Sit on the beach until Sophie gets there. God knows you could use a break. Just be sure to make fun of her new husband for me. 'Steven Stevens' is too funny." It's a name that sounds like it belongs to a cartoon dog carrying a briefcase.

"Are you sure? There's so much work to do and I feel bad—"

"You always feel bad and you never stop working. You're always here. Go, I'm fine. I can blast sixties music and walk around barefoot." She winks at me, teasing. Amy would dress like a flower child every day of the year. She taps a stack of papers on her desk and staples the corner. "Seriously, go. Have fun. Relax for a few days. Drink champagne and sleep with a stranger. You know, typical wedding stuff."

I laugh. "Typical for you, maybe."

Amy tips her head to the side, like she feels sorry for me. "You're twenty-two, Sky. You bust your ass every day and never stop to see what you're missing."

"Because I'm not missing a thing." I grab my purse from the desk drawer and push it shut. "Are you sure you're good here if I take off?" I never leave work early. If I haul ass, I can make the two o'clock ferry and get there with enough time to spend a few hours walking the beach or looking in the little shops.

Amy smirks, "Only if you promise to nail the best man for me." She waggles her eyebrows and clicks her tongue at me.

"Yeah. I'll do that," I say sarcastically, grabbing a shipping label and a marker from the desk drawer. Quickly, I scrawl, AMY WAS HERE across the envelope. "There ya go. I'll leave it on his forehead."

She laughs. "Bitch."

"No, crazy. I thought we established that."

As I push out the door, Amy yells, "Bring me some cake!"

"Will do!"

CHAPTER 3

By the time I get to the North Ferry at Orient Point, it's the middle of the afternoon. I change out of the suit I wear at the studio and trade it for a pair of faded jeans with a hole in the knee and a stretchy black tee shirt. I sit on the hood of my crappy old car, Big Red, and pull my dark hair into a ponytail. The wind is whipping it around, making it difficult to see. The truth is, I love the smell of the salt water and I love Shelter Island even more. Sophie's family maintains a summer home there, and since her parents were friends with my parents, we came out here with Sophie a lot. Sophie and I have been best friends since we were little. I don't really want to work her wedding, but she insisted that I do it.

Taking a deep breath, I look around. There are a few cars parked next to me, but since it's not summer anymore, the boat isn't full. Big Red is a rust-colored Bonneville that's older than I am. It sat in my grandpa's garage until he died last year. It's too big for the compact, modern parking spaces and was constructed back when gas was cheap and cars were huge. Grandpa used to complain about it being too small, which seems funny now. Both tires straddle the parking space. I used to have a motorcycle, but I had to sell it to make ends meet last month. Now it's just me and Big Red.

When we make it to the island, I follow the trail of cars off the boat and hit the road. I want to get checked in and make it to the other side of the island before Sophie arrives. I find the little inn that everyone is staying at and manage to parallel park. Who's awesome? Me! Maybe today won't suck after all. Horrible morning means a pleasant evening. I think I read that on a fortune cookie once.

Grabbing my purse, I head inside and go to the check-in counter. A woman with bright red hair and a black blazer is standing there with a phony smile on her clashing red lips.

"Welcome to the Chaucer Inn," she says. "How may I help you?"

God, she looks crazy. Her big green eyes don't blink and that creepy smile remains tightly in place. After glancing quickly around, I decide her boss must be nearby because something is making her uncomfortable and unnaturally still.

Placing my hands on the counter, I say, "Yes, I'm the photographer for the Stevens Wedding. I was told a room was reserved for me."

"Check in time isn't until 4pm."

"I know, but I hoped the room would be ready early. It was a long drive. Do you think you could help me out?"

She rolls her eyes and the smile fades. She breathes deeply, flaring her nostrils like a bull. "I am happy to help you find a seat at our restaurant until 4pm."

Did she not hear me? I tap my finger on the counter and lean in a little bit. "Is there any chance that I can have my room now? I'm really tired and—?"

"No! You can't have it now! It's not ready now! It'll be ready at 4pm! Are you hard of hearing or something?" The woman grips her side of the counter for a second and practically snarls.

Holy snails. That is the face of crazy. I smile with too many teeth and back away slowly. "I'll come back at 4pm."

The woman goes back to her unblinking, pleasantly possessed status. "That's a wonderful idea. Thank you so much. Enjoy your afternoon on Shelter Island."

OMG. What a nutter. I get out of the lobby before she sprouts claws and rips me to shreds. When I'm back out on the street, I decide to walk and grab a late lunch to kill the time. I'm sitting at a little bistro before I finally relax a little. My eye stops twitching, all thoughts of Nick and his assy ways long gone, and I'm content for once, sipping iced tea and nibbling on my sandwich. The little restaurant has all its seating outdoors on the sidewalk. The sky is blue and a slight breeze rustles through the branches. It's perfect.

Until my phone rings. It plays the Imperial March, aka Darth Vader's theme song, signaling that it's my mother calling. The guy next to me snorts his soda and looks over. I give a weak smile and slump back in my chair, letting it play the song again. Glancing at him, I explain, "It's my Mom."

He gives me a crooked grin. "She sounds amazing." The beautiful man returns to his meal with a smile on his face.

I swipe my finger across the screen and hold the evil little device to my ear. "Hey, Mom."

"Are you already out there? What happened at work today? You can't skip out just because you have somewhere fun to be." My mother thinks my job is a joke even though it more than paid the bills until Nick showed up. No one knows just how bad it's gotten and I sure as hell don't want to hear her lectures now.

"Mom, I didn't skip out. Amy is there."

"Amy won't do the same job you would do."

"Amy is stapling papers. I don't think she'll staple her hand too often, so we're okay. Have you and Daddy left yet?"

"Don't change the subject, Missy! I told you that you should have gone to college like Sophie did, but did you listen? No. Now, you run off in the middle of the day and leave Amy there alone. What if someone wants something?"

"Then they call me on my cell phone." Oh, God. Someone shoot me. I lean my cheek into my hand and lean sideways as Mom chews me out.

"That's no way to run a business, Sweetheart. Have you thought about what Daddy and I offered?"

"I'm not going to close my studio, Ma." My tilted body is off balance, as I perch on the side of my chair, ready to topple over. We've had this conversation too many times to count. They think I threw my life away because I didn't get a college degree. The thing is, all my friends who did are now jobless and flipping burgers. I don't have their debt and things were pretty good until Nick started screwing with me.

"Sophie is going to talk to you and I think you should listen to her."

My feet are crossed at the ankle. When she says that, I push too hard on my right foot and try to sit up quickly, but I must be standing on my shoelaces because my foot doesn't move. So, instead of going up, I fall down.

Picture a penguin at the zoo that suddenly falls sideways. Boop. It's really funny, except when I fall, my hands dart out and grab the closest thing to me—the guy at the next table. I manage to clutch a fist full of crotch and grope him thoroughly before hitting the cement. If he hadn't been facing me with his legs splayed like that, it wouldn't have happened. I was trying to grab the chair and totally missed.

The guy's eyes go wide and he jumps up, bumping the table with his hip. His pasta dish and tea start to slide as gravity pulls everything downward. By this time, I'm on the ground and I turn just in time to get a plate of spaghetti in the face, followed by a full glass of tea to wash it off.

I can hear my mother shrieking from somewhere on the sidewalk, still scolding me. For a moment, no one says anything. They just watch in horrified silence. I wipe the sauce and tea from my face and glance down. It looks like I was the victim of an assassination attempt by a clown. There's a huge red stain over my boobs with limp noodles in my hair, and a few hanging from the neckline of my shirt. One noodle is actually caught in my necklace. The tea diluted the sauce, which then ran into every crevice of my body, so I'm saucy and sticky. Not to mention, I groped a random stranger and knocked his table over.

I sit there way too long, trying to blink the stinging sensation out of my eyes. When I look up, the guy has his hand out. I take it and he helps me up.

"I am so sorry," he says. He isn't laughing at me, which comes as a shock.

"No, it was my fault," I say. Someone hands me my phone and I hit END

CALL without telling my mom goodbye. She calls back two seconds later.

Handsome guy chuckles at the Imperial March as it plays again. "I suggest not answering that."

I laugh, otherwise I'd cry. "Not planning on it."

The wait staff bustles around us, righting his table and cleaning up my mess, leaving the two of us standing awkwardly in the middle of the restaurant. "My name's Deegan, by the way. Deegan Greene. I'm a Sci-Fi nerd and I'm pretty sure you're a goddess."

A shy smile passes over my face, as I look at the ground and then back up at him. I hold out my sticky hand. "Sky Thompson."

"Can I walk you back to your hotel, Sky?"

"That depends. Is it four o'clock, yet?"

His jaw drops slightly. "Are you here for the Steve Stevens wedding, too?" The way he says it makes me laugh even though his lunch is stuck to my body.

"Yeah. How'd you know?"

"I'm guessing we had the same receptionist. I'm Steve's best friend."

I nod and pull a piece of spaghetti from my shirt. "I'm the photographer."

"Really?" I don't know why he says it like that. Apparently, I made a really bad impression, as if I'm too clumsy to photograph people.

"Yeah. I've known Sophie since we were kids."

"Ah, well then. We have a lot of catching up to do. I'm pretty sure if we put our heads together, we can thoroughly embarrass them." He winks at me and takes my elbow, before dropping enough cash for both of us on the table. "Steven had an unnatural love of glue. I'd hoped he'd have aspirations to take over the company that makes sticky-notes when he grew up."

I laugh a little. "It must have been a disappointment to see him become a pediatrician."

"Indeed. Come on. Let's see if we can get Satan's Spawn to let us check in. If she refuses, you should go sit on that big white chaise in the center of the lobby. I bet they'll change their mind about that four o'clock policy."

CHAPTER 4

Deegan is right. My room isn't ready until I say I am happy to wait and walk over to the little white couch. At that point, Spawny magically appears, room key in hand, and tosses my ass out of the lobby.

Deegan walks me to my room, helping me carry my bags and gear. After unlocking the door and tossing everything on the bed, he smiles at me. "Later, I will buy you a drink—or five—to make up for this."

His attention feels nice. Life has been too crazy to flirt with anyone in a long time. I smile crookedly. "I was the idiot who knocked your table over."

"I know, which is why it's horrible that I am still pristine and you are not." He winks at me and leaves before I can blush.

What a horrible how-we-met story. *Mom, this is Deegan. I grabbed his package at the sidewalk bistro down the street. It was good for both of us, until the food fell on my face.* Oh, God. In a split-second decision, I grab the doorknob and yank it open. "Deegan?" I poke my head out and see him waiting for the elevator.

He looks back at me. "Did you forget something?"

"Yeah, can we not tell anyone how we met?"

He smiles. "Ah, your mother doesn't know she's a Sith Lord?"

"Uh, she's evil incarnate, but no—not that. I mean, let's just say we met at check-in and leave everything else out." Meaning I'd rather not recap the fact that I've felt him up, uh, down in his nether regions.

He grins wickedly, but nods. "Of course. I'll see you later." He disappears

into the elevator and I slip back into my
room.

CHAPTER 5

Alone at last, and it's still half an hour before check-in. I have enough time to shower and get ready for tonight. Sophie is having a special dinner this evening for the wedding party and her closest relatives. It should be a week of fun with a camera strapped to my face—which is fine with me because I love shooting. Sophie and Steven will get married over the weekend and the guests will hang out for a few more days, because who wouldn't want to stay here? The place is beautiful, minus the demon at reception. Well, I think it's beautiful, but I bet Mom won't. We don't really get along very well.

My mother nearly had a stroke when I told her that I wouldn't be attending college. My brother and sister, both of whom are at least a decade older than me and perfect in every way, attended college. They were two perfect children, bestowed upon my darling parents from glorious angels above.

Blah, blah, puke. Seriously. You can't imagine what holidays are like at my parents' house. According to her, I'm obviously from the 'other side of heaven's tracks.' I love her, but we seriously don't see eye-to-eye—on anything. It's like, she got every parent's dream in kids one and two, so God thought it would be hysterical to throw Baby Oops at them a decade or so later, just to mix things up. Perfection comes in many shapes and sizes, but, to my mother, I'm not even close.

The perfect daughter would have a ring on her finger and be finishing college, while making arrangements for Barbie's dream summer wedding. I'm not that kid and Hell will have to freeze over before I let some douche put a ring on my finger. I may be mental, but after being up close and personal with the wedding industry for this long, I've seen things. Most couples get married because it's time, not because they're in love. They might have money issues, parental pressure, or they're simply tired of being alone—so they pick Mr. Good Enough and tie the knot.

That won't be me.

I head into the bathroom and turn on the shower, letting the tiny room get good and steamy before I shuck my clothes and get in. I sigh deeply and stand there, letting the water wash my troubles down the drain. If only life were this simple. I'd never leave the bathroom. I'm pretty sure if I put a fridge next to the tub, I could live in here. I'm half water rat, anyway.

My mind drifts to Sophie. I really hope she's making the right decision. We didn't get to talk about it. The engagement happened so fast and then she got swept away in planning a wedding. BAM! It got here faster than I thought it would. I wonder if she feels the same way. Rubbing my hands over my face, I sigh deeply and hope she's happy. Brides have a tendency to freak out. A serene bride is a medicated bride. Not only is a wedding the biggest commitment of someone's life, it's also the event with the highest probability of everything going wrong.

Example: the wedding I shot last weekend. The frosting shouldn't have caught fire like that, but it did. A few misplaced doilies, a strong gust of wind, and poof! Inferno cake. The little couple on top melted into little hunchbacks.

A wedding from earlier this month had an even more horrifying event: while the bride was walking down the aisle, her little flower girl got too close and stepped on her train. The sound of popping stitches filled the church, as a monster hole opened down the back of her gown, revealing the bride's panties—which were printed with the word BRIDE across her backside in Swarovski crystals. I was amazed when she just hugged the horrified flower girl and let someone staple the dress back together. That wedding continued, when most other brides would have eaten the entire assembly and spit out their bones for something like that. Never step on a bride, not unless you have a death wish.

A noise catches my ear, like someone is yelling down the hallway. I assume it's Sophie's younger cousins. After turning off the water, I step out and towel off. I look behind the door for a robe, but there isn't one. Whatever. I will not have a stroke and I have no plans to call the front desk for assistance, just to have Spawny bring me a robe that's been defiled. No thanks. I toss my wet towel on the edge of the tub and pad out of the bathroom naked. I head for my suitcase, which is on the bed, so I can grab my dress and make-up kit.

As I step through the bathroom door and into the room, I'm glancing at the dreadfully ugly carpet. It's like one of the Vegas-style, busy, rugs that hide every stain known to man. Damn, it's ugly. That's when I feel the sensation of eyes on me. The hairs on the back of my neck prickle at the same time a pair of shiny black shoes enter my field of vision. From there on, everything happens in slow motion. My entire body tenses as I lift my gaze.

Standing in front of me is Nick Ferro, ass-hat extraordinaire, with a huge smile on his face. "Don't tell me—you're the slutty bridesmaid."

I don't answer. I scream and try to cover up at least a little, so he can't see everything, but he already has. And the jerk is just standing there, with that amused grin on his face.

"Get out!" I scream the phrase over and over again, trying to hide both girls and wishing for a loincloth to magically appear in the proper place. Every time I grab one boob, the other falls out of my grip. They're too big to hold with one hand, but his eyes are all over me, and I don't want him looking. My hands move around spastically between my crotch and my chest, so I look like I'm landing a plane. For a second, I think about turning and running back into the bathroom, but then he'd see my butt, and since that's the one piece of me he hasn't seen, I refuse to turn around. Logic isn't one of my strong suits. Don't judge me until it happens to you. It makes sense. Sorta.

Nick steps back as I hurl the tissue box at him, and stumble backward into the bathroom. Nick says pleasantly, "This is my room. You get out."

"It's not your room, it's mine! I'm going to call the cops!" I bump into the sink and try to shove the door closed with my foot. It's an uberly uncoordinated effort that lands me on my ass. My ankle catches the door, closing it, as I not so gracefully fall backwards. I let loose a few expletives before a loud SLAM.

He rushes to the door. "And tell them what? That the guy you came on to didn't want you? I didn't say that, by the way." He's quiet for a second, and adds, "Are you all right?"

"No!" I'm not all right. Why is he here? Why is he in my room? This is the person responsible for singlehandedly destroying my business. Amy thinks I'm paranoid, but what the hell is he doing here, then? He shouldn't be here. I'm sitting with my back against the tub when the door cracks open. I kick it closed. "Oh my God! What kind of deviant are you? I didn't say come in!" My voice is at least an octave higher by the time I finish yelling at him.

"You said you weren't all right."

"I'm fine! Go away!"

"I can't. This is my room and I have a wedding to shoot this week, so if you don't mind—"

What? Scrambling to my feet, I grab the shower curtain and pull it off the rod. As I march out, the little plastic rings drag on the floor. Yanking the door open, I rush through and slam into his chest. I swear to God, my entire body made that dong sound that happens when you run into a metal pole. Not that I've done that. Recently. Oh holy hell, his body is hard. Why does he have to be so infuriatingly sexy? And he smells good, too. Meanwhile, I'm wet, sporting a rat's nest on my head, and styling the latest fashion in hotel shower curtains, which is that white plastic crap that sticks like tape to my damp skin.

I step back, but Nick steadies me, or I would have fallen over again. I don't say thank you. I want to bite his head off. "What wedding? No you don't!"

He speaks way too calmly. "Yes, I do. Mr. Stevens hired me."

What a liar. "He did not!"

Nick gives me that magical crooked smirk again and reaches into his gear bag, producing a wedding contract for photography services. I snatch it out of his hands and scan the thing. How could Sophie do this to me? I glance at him from the corner of my eyes, grinding my teeth. I'm very feminine when I'm pissed. I know. I flip to the last page and see a signature from Steven's Dad. "I'm sorry, Miss Thompson, but this is my wedding. You'll have to leave. Unless, I was right about my first guess and you're in the wedding."

"I'm not the slutty bridesmaid!" I smack the contract into his chest and stomp over to my bag, ripping out my contract with Sophie. I thrust it at him, spewing, "See! I'm the photographer and my contract says the same damn thing yours does!"

He reads it over and his jaw tightens, before he looks up at me with those annoyingly beautiful eyes again. Where the hell did they come from? Those blue eyes sparkle so much it looks like dwarves mined them or something. "I guess it does." He shrugs. "Apparently, we were both hired to photograph the same event, and we were both given the same room—the photographer's room."

"Over my dead body."

CHAPTER 6

I shove past him and make a beeline for the elevator. Nick follows after me with his gear bag still on his shoulder and an aggravating smile across that sexy face. I'm starting to appreciate why Mrs. Getty hired him. The guy is eye candy from head to toe.

There's an awkward moment when we both step into the elevator and I notice that I ran out of the room wearing a rather transparent shower curtain. It was better than being naked, but not by much. Nick presses his lips together like he's trying not to laugh. Asshole.

The bell chimes and the doors open. I haul my butt across the room and shove to the front of the line at the reception desk. Spawny is still there and her eyes widen when she sees me. I slam my hand on the counter, jab my thumb back at Nick and say, "Did you seriously give a strange man a key to my room?"

"He said he was the photographer." She doesn't blink.

"I'M THE PHOTOGRAPHER!"

Nick is standing there behind me, and turns his charm up to levels that only magical creatures can manage, before bursting into glitter. "I think there's been a mix up and I'm happy to purchase another room." He puts his key card on the counter and flashes a dazzling white smile at Spawny.

The wicked witch visibly shudders and taps her computer keys, before looking up apologetically. "I'm sorry, sir, but there aren't any other rooms available."

Nick's voice tightens. "None?"

She shakes her frizzy red mane. "I'm sorry, sir."

He looks back at me. "We'll just have to share. Thank-you, Miss. Your service is wonderful. If I can fill out a comment card, just let me know." He winks at her and leaves.

WTF? That did not just happen. Spawny has a girlish smile on her evil face and her gaze follows after Nick. She totally ignores me for a second, then turns and shoots imaginary lava out of her eyeballs until I leave.

As I clatter across the wooden lobby floors, I hear a familiar voice. "Skylar Thompson! Is that you?"

I turn and smile at my friend. "Sophie Soon-to-be-Stevens!" I give her a little hug and then she points at my outfit.

"Uh, dinner is casual, but I think we might need to define that a little bit better. I'd hoped you'd be wearing some clothes." Sophie looks good. Her skin has that sun-kissed look that goes with her olive complexion and rosy cheeks. The lavender dress she's wearing has a form-fitting bodice and flares right above the knee. She looks perfect.

And I'm wearing a shower curtain. Good God, I hope my mother isn't here yet.

"Ha ha." I don't want to dump extra stuff on her, but I have to tell her. "Did you know Steven's Dad hired another photographer?"

Her smile falters. "Oh crap." She sighs and pushes her hair out of her face, looking around the room as she does it. People are everywhere, hugging, saying hellos. Someone calls to Sophie and she waves back. "I was afraid he'd do that. I told him my friend was shooting the wedding and he said he wanted a professional. I told him that you were a professional, but I guess he didn't believe me. He kept talking about his friend's daughter's wedding and green pictures. I don't know exactly what happened, but he kept saying he didn't want that to happen at our wedding. Is it a problem?" Worry pinches her pretty little face and I feel like a jerk for saying anything.

Smiling at her, I shake my head. "No. I'll work it out."

"Good, because I'm not letting someone else do the bridal boudoir pictures of me in sexy poses—especially not some old guy with a camera." She shivers like it'd be creepy.

"I'll still do everything we agreed on. Don't worry about it, Sophie. We'll work it out. Just enjoy yourself."

She grins at me and looks through the sea of people, spying Steven. Her smile broadens as her ribcage fills with air. "I can't believe it's finally here." She squees and skips away, still Sophie after all these years.

For a second, I stand there watching the two of them together. That's when I hear her voice over my shoulder.

"What on earth are you wearing? Really, Skylar, I brought you up better than this!"

Resisting the urge to roll my eyes, I turn on my heel. "Hello, Mother."

"I really think you should talk to Dr. Norman about medication dear."

Oh, screw it. My eyes roll up and I push two fingers to my temple, attempting to ease the sudden pain.

"We've been through this, Mom. I'm not crazy."

"Well, did you get locked out of your room?"

"No." Her perfect eyebrow lifts and she taps one shiny red patent leather shoe on the floor. I smile serenely and pull at the curtain. "This is my dinner dress."

She thinks I'm serious. "Well, go change. You can't wear that monstrosity. Sophie will be horrified."

"Sophie already saw me, Ma."

"Well, then she's much too kind. You look insane. Go change." She turns away from me and greets a stranger with more warmth than she just gave me.

Working my jaw, I pad across the polished floor to the elevator and shoot laser beams from my eyes at the doors, willing them to open.

The couple next to me looks seriously worried, so I glance over at them and smile. "Hey." I nod, like I'm normal. "What's up?"

The woman is older than me, maybe fortyish, and tries to smile politely, but I think I broke her face, because it twitches.

The guy she's with acts like I'm the poster child for normal. Ha. He should inform my mother, because she's probably in the chapel looking for holy water.

The doors open and we all walk in. I turn and press the button for my floor. Looking up, I see my mother across the room and a horrified expression clouds her normally placid face. I wave the tips of my fingers and smile as the doors shut.

This week is going to suck.

CHAPTER 7

I don't have my key card. I left it with Spawny downstairs. Super suck. When I get to my door, I knock. I know he's in there. Nick disappeared from the lobby way before me and I would have seen him through the massive amount of floor-to-ceiling glass windows downstairs.

A second later, he pulls the door open. Nick has his cell phone pressed to his ear. "Are you sure? Nothing? All right, thank you so much." How does he do that? It always sounds like he's so nice, but the man is a snake. He destroys everything he touches, like one of those demigods in Amy's stories.

Nick runs his hand through his dark hair and tosses the phone on the bed next to my bags. "Well, it looks like we're roomies. Every other place on the island is booked solid and no one has an extra room. So much for small town life, huh?"

My jaw opens and I make a repulsive face without thinking. "You are not staying with me."

"Yeah, I think the sentence you're looking for is, 'thank you for not throwing me out on my ass.'" His eyes dip to my butt. The shower curtain clings tightly and I'm pretty sure I have a wedgie. I'm losing it. My lower left eyelid twitches and the more I try to steady it, the worse it gets. Nick sits on the bed and lays back. Staring at the ceiling, he asks, "Your head isn't going to spin in circles is it? If so, let me know and I'll sit up and watch."

Every muscle in my body is corded tight. The mental strings that tie this hot mess together are coming undone and all I can manage to do is stand here mashing my lips together. When I finally speak, my body is vibrating with DEFCON 5 cray-

cray. "I hate you." Holy understatement, Batman.

"Really?" He has the audacity to sound surprised. Nick lifts his head and looks at me with that stupid smile on his face.

"Yes, really! You're destroying my business and ruining my life! What the hell is wrong with you? Why can't you get hit by lightning or something? God knows you deserve it."

He shrugs and lies back down. "He can't smite something this awesome. Besides, then who would be left to ruin your life?"

"Don't mock me. We both know what you're doing. Don't pretend to be stupid and charming with me. It won't work."

"What if I just opt for charming?"

"Asshole."

"I call dibs on the bed, by the way," he says without looking up. "I might as well live up to the accusations."

"I was here first, so the bed is mine. You can sleep in the hallway." I don't want to open my bag in front of him—I packed some nice panties in there and they're right on top. Weddings are full of surprises and I didn't want to have grannies on if things took a turn for the best. Obviously, that's not going to happen, but I still need to get my clothes out, while holding up the shower curtain, and hiding way too many lacy, thongy things. I manage to get the suitcase unzipped and shove a hand inside.

Nick has his hands behind his head. He looks over at me. "You're cute when you're mad. Did you know that?"

"Your life expectancy will significantly decrease if you sleep in here tonight."

"You should really go home."

"You should really cancel your contract and stop stalking me."

"I'm not leaving."

"Well, neither am I. Sophie's my friend and I promised her some things. I'll be damned if I let you shove me out." Where the hell is my dress? My fingers loop around the strap. Finally. It should be right under the mountain of panties, so I give it a quick tug with one hand while holding the curtain up with the other.

Two words: underwear everywhere.

It's like a panty explosion in a rainbow of colors. The little lacy bottoms go flying, as the dress emerges from my bag. Several pairs land on Nick's face. I press my eyes shut and try not to scream. Jumping up and down and yelling won't help. It won't.

Nick sits up and suppresses a grin, as he peels panties off his face. He holds up a pair of satin butterfly bottoms and sticks his fingers through the opening, looking impressed. "Are you sure that you're not the slutty bridesmaid? Because these crotchless babies are just the kind she'd wear."

I snatch them away and shove them into my bag. "The slutty bridesmaid doesn't wear panties at all, jackass. Damn, how many weddings have you shot? She's not wearing anything but her dress, and will flash her titties at you later. You go to her room for the night and I'll push you off a cliff tomorrow. I hope you have worker's comp." Translation: Go to Hell.

Nick actually laughs. Wonderful. The guy has a death wish. As I disappear into the bathroom, he calls out, "Are you sure you don't take meds?"

"I hate you!" I yell through the door.

"Yeah," he mumbles, "you covered that part already."

What the hell am I supposed to do with this? I press my head to the closed door and try to calm down, but I can't. I have to live with the man who's destroying my life for the next five days, while also trying to convince my mother that I made the right career choice. This was supposed to be my opportunity to show off my mad skills, not have some lowlife complicate everything.

Two people can't be in control of one wedding, which is why there's a non-compete clause in my contract. But it's too late now. I can't tattle to Sophie without causing tension between her and her father-in-law, and I don't want to do that. That leaves me only one option.

I have to kick Nick Ferro's ass in every conceivable way.

CHAPTER 8

When I emerge from the bathroom, my dress is zipped up and my hair is done. I don't want to see Nick again, but it's not like I can hide forever. I glance around quickly and find him standing near the window with his phone pressed to his ear.

His voice drifts inside. He sounds defensive, like he's trying to convince someone of something. "I already have. Listen, it's a business move, pure and simple. I'm on target to have the task completed before the deadline, and I expect you to hold up your end of the bargain." His back tenses as he listens to the response. He must suck in a breath and hold it because his ribs expand, but don't contract. Nick shakes his head and I can see his jaw is locked tight, like he's holding back his thoughts.

Nick must feel my gaze, because he looks over his shoulder and sees me. His voice drops, but I can still hear him. "Yes, sir. Listen, I can't talk now. I'll fill you in later. Thank you." He disconnects and turns around. "Do you always eavesdrop?"

"You're in my room and talking way too loud, so, yeah. I heard you." I'm sitting on the edge of the bed and slipping into a pair of black heels. "By the way, get over yourself. Like I care what you think or do." My hair slips over my shoulder as I put on the second shoe. When I look up, Nick has a strange expression on his face. "What?"

"You're seriously going to work wearing heels? What if they want to go down by the beach? There are rocks everywhere. You'll break your neck." Nick is standing at the foot of the bed with his hands in his pockets. It's an honest question, but I'm not taking anything at face value with this guy.

Pushing up from the mattress, I walk over to him. With my fuck-me heels on we stand eye-to-eye. I smile and laugh lightly. It sounds a little evil. "Listen, I know I've shot more weddings than you, and, since you copy everything I do, I know that you can't come up with a single idea on your own. The way I see it, you should put on a pair of heels and kiss my ass. Maybe you'd actually learn something and you wouldn't have to be a monkey with a camera anymore." Harsh much? Maybe, but the guy is a dick. He totally has it coming, and I'm not holding back.

His lips curl into a playful smile. "Are you suggesting that you're a better photographer than I am?"

"I'm not suggesting it, I'm saying it. You're shooting second this week. Stay out of my way." When a team of photographers offers coverage for a single event, there's a main shooter—called first—and a secondary shooter. The person shooting second is typically less experienced and can't nail the shots needed to shoot as first shooter. It's a slam at his ability.

"I am not shooting second." Nick inches closer so he's in my face. "If you think that I'm going to hand over this wedding to you, you're mistaken."

I laugh lightly and tip my head to the side. "How cute. You think you have a choice in the matter."

His warm breath slips across my cheek as he speaks. "I do, and if you get in my way, you're going to wish you hadn't."

I press the end of his nose like a button, which seems to shock him. "We'll see about that." I turn on my heel, grab my gear bag, and head toward the elevator feeling like I handled that very well. I suck at confrontation. Stuff always goes totally screwy and I usually end up making things worse.

While I'm waiting for the doors to open, Nick appears in a black jacket and dark jeans. He looks like a freaking rock star. If Sophie acts like a Ferro groupie and swoons because Nick is at her wedding, I'm going to lose it. Nick is all charm and smiles again as he steps next to me, camera in hand.

"You forgot something," I say without looking at him. Like all his gear. What the hell is he going to do with one camera?

"I don't need multiple bodies," he says it seductively. When I glance at him, he winks. "When I find something I like, I tend to be monogamous. I'm satisfied with one camera and a good lens."

Another couple materializes from the room next door and steps into the elevator with us. They're dressed for dinner, so I assume they're also going to Sophie's wedding. The old woman has silvery hair cut short and styled in that poodle hairdo grannies typically sport. She smiles at me. "Are you the photographer for Sophie's wedding?"

Holding out my hand, I smile as she takes it. "Yes I am. Sky Thompson from Bella Chicks studio."

"Is this handsome young man your beau?"

I nearly choke. Nick thrusts his hand past me. "Nick Ferro from Bella Clicks studio."

"So your studios work together?"

"Yes," Nick replies.

"No," I say at the same time and then glare at him. The doors open and the old couple walks out, wishing us well. After they're out of earshot, which is like two steps, I hiss at him. "Don't tell people that we're working together."

He shrugs. "Fine, just trying to save you from embarrassment."

"Yeah, I'm sure." I roll my eyes and walk away from him, but the guy stays glued to my heels.

"So, nepotism, huh?"

"Bite me, Ferro."

"Later, Sky." Before I can reply, he disappears into the crowded lobby.

CHAPTER 9

I try to stop mashing my lips together, so I don't get labeled as the crazy girl, but I think the shower curtain dress kind of did that for me. People smile carefully at me and leave a wide berth as they pass.

I find the room where dinner is being served, pull out my camera and slap on my 20mm lens. After adjusting the camera settings, I get to work photographing all the little details in the room before everyone arrives.

I have my camera to my face when I hear Daddy's voice. "Tell me that the crazy woman in the shower curtain everyone is talking about wasn't my daughter." He's standing in the doorway with a big smile, his hands tucked into his pockets. He seems so old and fragile compared to my mother. As a child, I thought my Dad could rule the world and save me from anything, well, anything except my mother. He holds out his arms. "Get over here."

I step into his arms and feel his hands pat my back, before he pulls away just enough to kiss my cheek. "Hey Dad."

"Are you all right? You haven't called in a while. Do you have enough money? Here." He pulls a fifty dollar bill from his pocket and shoves it in my hands.

I try to give it back, but he won't let me. "I'm fine Dad." Lie number one, but I want it to be true so it's not like I'm going to burn in Hell for misleading him. Besides, I want him to be proud of me. I've made something successful from nothing, well, until Nick came along, that is.

"No, you're not. Tell me what's going on. Why were you wearing a shower curtain?"

"Mr. Stevens hired another photographer. Neither of us knew about it until we got here."

"Is it a problem?"

Yes, but I can't tell him that. I want him to relax and have fun. He doesn't need to be worrying about me. "I can work around it. It was just unexpected, that's all."

"You're a good girl, Sky. I haven't told you enough, but I'm proud of you. That little shop you put together is great—and you did it on your own. Your mother had a fit, but I think she's finally getting used to the idea that you can be successful without college."

Oh God. It's like he reached into my chest, grabbed my heart, and twisted. I thought I'd die before I ever heard my mother's approval. I turn away and hold the camera to my face, before bending over to shoot a place card with Sophie's name on it. "Thanks, Dad."

"You should come around more, Sky."

"I will, Dad." There's a knot in my throat. I'll have to come around more because everything is falling apart. I'm not going to clear rent this month. Nick stole too many of my clients. I barely have enough money to pay Amy. I keep thinking that if I work hard and play fair, good things will happen. And that was true for a little while. I had a steady flow of clients, until Nick showed up.

Speak of the Devil. Nick Ferro walks into the room and also starts shooting. Daddy walks over to him. Panic shoots through me. Parents only ever do one of two things—gush about their children or threaten people who are screwing with their kids. "Are you the other photographer?"

Nick turns and looks at my Dad. "Yes sir."

"Do a good job. Sophie's like a daughter to me and like a sister to Sky. I was worried we wouldn't have any pictures of the two of them together. Make sure you take some." Daddy slips away before Nick has a chance to reply.

I don't look at him. I won't apologize for being friends with Sophie or for my Dad's statement. I'd also worried there would be no pictures of Sophie and me together, and it bothers me that the solution to that problem is Nick Ferro.

Nick glances over his shoulder at me. "Your Dad?"

"Yeah." I say, as I lift the eyepiece to my face and take another shot.

"He cares about you." Nick says it and then goes back to shooting, like it surprises him that my Dad gives a flying flip about me.

I'm not sure if it's a jab—I don't see how it could be—but it feels off. We don't speak and soon I have all the shots I need and text Sophie asking when she plans to walk into the room. I want to get a picture of the look on her face when she sees this.

Everything is so pretty. Elegant white linens embellished with lace and the palest blue ribbons cover each table. The centerpieces are tall sprigs of white branches, little crystals hanging artfully on their delicate twigs. The silvery band on the edge of each plate perfectly complements its accompanying sterling flatware and crystal goblets. The space where Sophie and Steve will sit is flooded with golden light from the setting sun. I already have some ideas that will look stunning, assuming Nick isn't in my way. I'm not sure what to do if he is.

————

The meal goes smoothly. There's an awkward part where Mr. Stevens comes up to me and apologizes profusely for hiring another photographer.

"I had no idea that you owned your own studio. Sophie said you were a friend, so I thought—"

"Don't worry about it," I smile. "And just think, now you'll have twice as many pictures."

Mr. Stevens looks like his son, with the exception of his salt and pepper hair. There are black streaks by his temples, but the rest is white and thinning on top. His big brown eyes are sincere and I know he feels sheepish. Weddings bring out everyone's temper, and he keeps telling me that he didn't want to hurt my feelings. The man truly meant well. I wouldn't want a hobbyist shooting this wedding either. It's a lighting nightmare and someone with lesser skills would have gotten nonstop crap.

"You're such a sweet girl," Mr. Stevens adds before allowing me to wander away and get more shots.

Sunlight is pouring through the window behind Sophie and Steve, forming a nice little halo known as a rim light. It's perfect. I move around the edge of the room, smiling at people as I go. A few of Sophie's aunts paw at me as I pass. "Sit down and eat something, Sky. You've hardly had a bite all night."

"I will, right after I get this shot." I wink at them and pass, heading to a spot nearly directly across from the bride and groom-to-be. After metering the light, I'm thrilled. It's exactly what I wanted. Now I just have to camp out here until they kiss. I'll have a perfect silhouette, surrounded by a nice soft glow.

While waiting, I'm sitting at a table with people on either side. They keep asking to borrow my camera so they can take a shot. Who does that? I mean, no one asks the dentist to give the drill a go. There's this perception that anyone can shoot a picture, that the camera is the brain of the operation, however a camera couldn't shoot this. I'm in full manual mode and have carefully adjusted all my settings so the finished product will look perfect. It always amuses me when people ask what I shoot with, as if that's what makes the images look good. The truth is, photography requires skill and practice. Photography is art. Even if you have a good eye, you have to know how to control the camera to make the images look the way you want.

Speaking of people who think chimps could shoot weddings, here comes my mother. She commandeers the empty chair next to me, sits and whispers softly, "You look ridiculous sitting there with the camera covering your face. If you don't know what you're doing, at least try and project professionalism, Skylar."

My jaw tenses and I bite my tongue, but when I don't move, she doesn't leave. The camera is still resting on my cheek while I lean my elbows on the table, waiting for the shot. "I am a professional, Mom."

"Well, it looks like you're confused, darling. Take your picture already." Finally, she gets up and leaves. Thank God.

Sophie's head tips towards Steven's, but they haven't kissed yet. My shot is almost there. I want a picture of a stolen kiss; the way people kiss when they think no one is paying attention. It looks like I'm shooting the floor from here with the way my lens is angled down. It's stealth mode. Make the bride and groom think you're shooting something else and they'll act normal. Otherwise you end up with tons of cheeser pictures. Whoever told little kids to say cheese and smile should be shot.

Nick takes the empty spot next to me. "What are we looking at?"

"Nothing, troll, now wander away." I don't want him to copy me. Call it childish, but it's my shot and I want to be the only one to have it.

"Ouch. You don't play fair, Miss Thompson."

"Neither do you, Mr. Ferro, but you don't see me complaining."

He smirks and leans back in his chair. Don't look up. Don't look up. If he has any artistic eye at all, he'll see the perfect triangulation of the couple and perfection of the light. Nick places his camera on the table. "I won't steal your shot. Satisfied?"

I don't look over at him, but I can see him out of the corner of my eye. "No, but go back to Babylon and ask me again. My answer might change."

"I doubt it."

"Yeah, me too, but it was worth a try."

He smiles and glances over at me. "So, let's pretend you don't hate my guts for a second. What pose are you waiting for? Because all I see is garish lighting." I want to tell him, because it's always fun to talk shop, but I don't want to risk it. "Oh, come on, Sky. I'm not even holding my camera. Tell me what you're waiting for and I'll help you get your shot."

Glancing over at him, I say, "I need them to kiss. I'll show you after I take it, okay?"

"Deal." He winks at me and pushes out of his seat. Nick moves over a few seats and whispers to someone. I have no idea what he said, but a ruckus of loud laughter breaks out a few seconds later. Everyone is looking that way, except Steven. Instead, his eyes are caressing Sophie's cheek, waiting for her to turn back to him. I pretend to fiddle with my camera, and a moment later, she turns. They're drawn together like magnets. That's when I press the button and the camera shutter clicks, but no one can hear it over the noise at the other end on the table. Sophie smiles warmly at Steven and rests her forehead against his. They exchange a few whispered moments, unaware that anyone is watching. It's perfect.

When I finally pull my camera away from my face and stand, I see Nick at the other end of the table flanked by two of Steven's cousins, singing very loudly and swaying. I can't even tell what song it is. As I inch closer, I see my mother making a horrible face and slip into the empty seat next to my father. "What song is that?"

"They're singing three songs at once. Nick bet them that they couldn't carry a tune as long as he could. They started with four, and it looks like Max is about to mess up." A moment later Max says the wrong word, matching Nick, and curses loudly before sitting down.

"The wedding photographer should not sing," my mother says over her shoulder.

"Don't worry, I'm not." Mom turns around again and the two remaining men manage another few notes before Nick winks at me.

He fumbles his tune and laughs loudly. "You won," he gushes. "This guy beat me!" Nick goes on and on about how no one has ever bested him, as everyone claps. Sophie is giggling, watching them, and leans in to say something to Steven.

Nick manages to sneak out of the crowd and become a wallflower again. How does he do that? I'm leaning against the wall across from Sophie when he slips next to me. "So, let's see it. What'd I make an ass out of myself for?"

I hold up my camera so he can see. Nick's jaw literally drops and he slowly reaches for my camera. Since the strap is around my neck, I go where the camera goes. Turning, I stand way too close to him and unhook it from my neck. "Here," I hand him the camera. "You don't have to kill me to see it."

He doesn't speak for a moment, staring at the image. "Okay, how did you do this?"

I smirk. "Trade secret."

"Oh come on, at least give me a hint."

Taking my camera back, I shake my head. "What? And give you more ways to put me out of business? I don't think so." I wander away, not expecting him to follow, but he does. There's nothing left to shoot, but I keep shooting so I don't have to talk.

"You keep saying that."

"Because you keep doing it."

"What exactly am I doing?" Oh God, his blue eyes are hypnotic.

I look away. "You stole three clients from me this month."

His voice is warm and playful. "It's just business, Sky."

"Not when you attack every folder-holding-person who walks out of my store. What'd you offer them, cookies if they came inside?"

He steps in front of me, but I don't stop walking until he's there. So, I basically crash into him, my camera still in front of my face. "Trade secret." He winks at me.

I roll my eyes and shoulder past him. "You're a dick. Find your own clients and stop stealing mine." I worked so damn hard to get those people into my studio and all he has to do is snake them when they walk back out. Meanwhile, I'm the one who paid for the ads and worked my ass off at shows and bridal expos to get them there.

He stops following me, but I can feel his eyes on my back. "You're talented."

I hold up my camera like I belong on a Wheaties box. Whatever. Like talent even matters anymore. Although, it's nice to hear him say it. This industry is overrun with people who don't know what they're doing. I've heard a million sob-stories from brides after the fact: 'my pictures are blurry,' 'my photographer didn't show up,' 'everyone is green.' It's hard not to laugh at the last one. Screwed up white balance makes everything the wrong color. It's the error of a novice. Sophie and Steven's wedding has difficult shooting conditions, but I'm looking forward to the challenge. When I glance back at Nick, he's gone.

CHAPTER 10

I linger at the dinner long after everyone else is gone. It's part of evading my mother—The Plan. It sounds more dramatic that way and, since she makes everything dramatic, it suits her. She left with the rest of the guests a while ago. I said I was lingering to check lighting conditions in the chapel and outside. It's a total lie, but I don't want to go back to the room yet either. Nick gets under my skin so badly I want to burn him off. Ferro brat.

I wander out of the main building. The grounds of the hotel are sprawling. They take up a good chunk of the island. Since the sun has set, and there are only scattered landscaping lights, it's pretty dark. I'm not concerned—not the way I would be in the city. Walking through Manhattan's streets after midnight, alone, loaded with gear is stupid. I currently have over two grand worth of camera stuff on my body. And that's my new net worth: whatever's on my body. I don't know how to tell Amy that I'm going to need to let her go. Oh, God, I'm going to have to let Amy go.

The salty air blows gently across my cheeks, lifting my hair, and I wish time could freeze. I'd live out here if I could. Places like Shelter Island resemble little coastal towns from a hundred years ago, but with modern luxuries.

As I walk along the gravel path toward the chapel, I look for good places to shoot Steve and Sophie. What I really want are pictures of them down by the water, on the rocks, with the sea spray around them. I could take the photo at night and use the moon as a rim light, so that it illuminates their outline ever so slightly. It'd be so romantic, but it's also certain to trash her dress. I have some brides that like the idea of messing up their gown for a cool picture, but Sophie isn't one of them.

I press the eyepiece to my face and snap the shot. When I pull the camera away, I can tell how beautiful it would be. It's the kind of picture that is the memory. Everyone would want it. It's packed with emotion and has so much vivid detail it's hard not to feel the spray of the sea on your skin or smell the salty water.

I walk over to the massive boulders along the shore, climb to the top of the slick rock, and sit down. The night breeze is cool and feels good against my flesh. It was so stuffy inside that my shirt is still sticking to my back.

Tipping my head back, I glance up at the stars, wishing that I could fly away. I never grew up. I still hope and dream for things that aren't within my reach. I don't want to accept the life my mother tries to shove down my throat over and over again. I want to live by the seat of my pants and build my life my way, on my terms, not hers.

Speak of the devil. In the silence of the night, my phone blares the Imperial Death March. I don't bother answering. This is a perfect spot and I'm not tarnishing it with the memory of her chiding voice. Aiming my camera at the bay, I rest it against my knee and change the shutter speed. It's insanely slow now. I line up the shot and press the button. The responding click of the shutter is slow to come, and I'm careful not to move. I have the reputation for having a super steady hand. A shot turns blurry for most people around $1/80^{th}$ of a second. I can hand hold a camera at $1/10^{th}$ of a second. The shutter stays open longer, allowing in more light. Though it appears to be pitch black, the sensor will pick up the subtle light lining the top of the waves, edging the soft clouds and emitting from scattered stars. I wish I could get Sophie out here.

The shutter clicks, completing the exposure before he speaks. "Hey SB. What are you doing out here all alone? Don't you have any sense? You could slip into the water and never be seen again."

Nick climbs up next to me and leans toward me, resting all his weight on one leg.

"SB?"

"Slutty bridesmaid."

I work my jaw before I speak. "I'm going to kill you. I'll push you in, I swear I will."

He grins and holds up his palms in surrender. "No reason to threaten me. If you want me to go, I'll go."

"Then go." My voice is stern. I don't look at him as he stands. I expect him to walk away, but he doesn't. Instead, Nick kicks off his shoes and darts past me, diving from the edge of the rock into the water below.

I scream and lean over the side of the rock edge with my camera dangling around my neck. Nick emerges from darkness, sheets of water pouring from his face. Taking his hands, he pushes his hair back and laughs.

I can't help it, I scream. A lot. "You stupid son of a bitch! You scared me! I thought you—"

Nick laughs. "Since when do you care? I believe your exact words were go jump off a cliff." He's treading water below.

"They were not! I said go, not jump, you idiot." After my heart resumes a normal pace I give him a half-smile and wonder why he did it.

"To make you loosen up," he answers as if he were a mind reader. "Come in."

"Psh, no. I don't think so." I look away and shake my head.

"Ah," he nods. "Too prude. I get it."

"How am I too prude if you nicknamed me SB?"

Shrugging, he disappears beneath the water. After a second, he comes up again and laughs. "It's warm, SB. Come on. You'll have fun."

I hesitate. Part of me wants to jump in—it's the same crazy part that thinks Neverland is real and believes fairies really do exist. They must, somewhere. But I hear my mother's voice and know that I should get back to Sophie. She wanted to talk to me. "Sorry, Ferro. You'll have to be crazy all by yourself." I smirk at him and unhook my camera from my neck.

I've just set it down and am fishing for the lens cap in my dress pocket, when I feel his fingers wrap around my ankle.

"Don't you dare." I try to dig my heel in, but it's too late. Nick already tugged. I fall, feet first, and plunge into icy cold water. When I come up gasping, he's next to me. I screech and punch his shoulder. "You asshole! You said it was warm!"

Nick's laughing, watching me like I'm a mermaid about to disappear. "If I had told you it was freezing you would never have come in."

"I didn't come in! You pulled me in!"

"Same difference." He shrugs, and takes my hands, pulling me away from the rock. "Can you swim?"

"I'd be dead if I couldn't." The hem of my dress keeps floating up and I'm wearing a G-string. It's cute and black and matches my bra, but I don't want him to see it. The further out we swim, the closer we get to the patch of moonlight. "Nick, wait."

"We're almost there. I want to show you something."

I humor him and follow, half treading water and half pulling my dress down as it floats up to my boobs. Nick notices, but averts his eyes, which surprises me. Tugging my wrist, he pulls me to the center of the reflection of the moon on the water. "Look at the shore."

When I turn back, I gasp. It's the most stunning thing I've ever seen. Although I've been here many times as a child, Sophie and I never came out here at night. We weren't allowed to wander from the shore. As I move my arms back and forth over the top of the water, I gaze at the hotel and the rocks bathed in the palest moonlight you've ever seen. It looks like a painting. The way the soft light glitters off the water makes me think of old fairy tales and happier times.

My teeth chatter louder the longer we're there. Nick waits a moment and then adds, "Wouldn't it be great if we could get Sophie and Steven out here."

"Yeah, but she won't come. She doesn't want to ruin her dress."

"And here you are, in a beautiful dress and up to your neck in water."

I glance at him for a second and tuck my damp hair behind my ear. "We're not the same. I like this kind of thing and the memory that it makes is priceless. She doesn't really get it, you know? There are some things that only come once in a lifetime, some places that are so pristine they seem like magic." I smile wistfully. Shelter Island was my Neverland. This place was where I was a girl with no worries, where I slipped away from reality to be myself for a while.

Nick nods, as if he understands, but I doubt it. I shiver again and when he turns, our eyes lock. My stomach flips when he looks at me like that. The pull to his mouth is so hard, it's as if we're connected. Our bodies move closer as his lashes lower. His beautiful blue eyes fixate on my lips, drifting closer and closer, he tips his head to the side for a kiss.

One kiss. It won't hurt anything. It means nothing.

His warm breath washes over my face and it aches to not close the gap between us. I want this, but I won't do it. I can't. He's the enemy. I'd be a traitor to myself if I let him in. There can never be anything between us, ever. That's just the way it is.

Just before our lips touch, I tuck my head and the kiss misses. Nick presses his lips together and inhales hard, while I fish something out of my pocket. It's been there, in my pocket, since the first time I came to Shelter Island. I grab the little piece of metal attached to a necklace, take his hand, press it into his palm, and close his fingers around it. "This is the only kiss you're getting from me."

It's symbolic to me. I've worn that thing forever, but I need to stop dreaming. It's time for things to change. As I start to swim back to the rock, he looks down into his hand and sees an old thimble.

This island was my Neverland and everything about it offered freedom—at least, every visit until now. Now, it's time to grow up, Sky. It's time to make my own magic.

In order to survive, Nick and I can't be friends. I have to make sure he's not at that rehearsal tomorrow.

CHAPTER 11

I take my time getting back to the room, even though I'm frozen. Nick is asleep in the bed, but he's made me a pallet on the floor from blankets and pillows. I jump in the shower, just standing there warming up, until my skin is scalded. Then I slip on a pair of sweats. I pad out of our room and down the hall to Sophie's room. It's after midnight. I leave my gear behind. I just want to talk to her and see if she's all right.

I knock on her door and it swings open. "Sky!" She throws her arms around me and clobbers me in a bear hug before pulling me inside. "I'm so glad you stayed.

I was afraid Nick Ferro would chase you off."

"Oh, no. I'm staying—Ferro or not. Besides, I'm a better shooter than him, by far."

One of the bridesmaids I don't know scoffs. "A little arrogant there, aren't you?"

My gaze cuts over to her. She has a pointy face and fake red hair. It looks like she went down on the Kool-Aid guy and he came in her hair. It's, like, holy fuck R.E.D. "Just calling it like I see it. If he were better than me, he wouldn't have to copy me. Besides, what do you know about it? Jack shit, that's what. So keep your mouth shut."

Kool Cum makes a face at Sophie and mutters, "Bitch."

"Excuse me?" I'm crossing the room and standing in front of her. The girl is wearing purple PJs and sitting on the floor with a bottle of wine in her hand. It's the little plastic kind the hotel sells downstairs.

"You heard me. You're a bitch—a deranged one from what I've heard." She smirks.

Sophie jumps between us. "And Mandy had too much to drink." She pulls the cup away from Mandy and laughs nervously.

"And I've had nothing to drink, so tell me, Mandy—what'd you hear about me that made you instantly hate my guts? Or is it just that you're the slut at this party, but Nick already has another woman in his room?"

Mandy lunges for me and I'm ready to punch her, but Sophie and another girl jump in the middle. Sophie screams, "Mandy stop it! Sky, I'm going to kill you!"

We're apart and I'm breathing hard. I press my fingers to my chest. "Me?"

"Yeah you. You're not drunk. She is."

"That's a shitty answer, Sophie."

"I've got an idea Conceited Chick will find interesting. I bet you that the best picture taken at this wedding is Nick Ferro's and not yours." Mandy smirks pointing a half-filled wine glass at me.

"Cut it out, Mandy." Sophie warns Kool Cum to back down, but she doesn't.

"Come on girls, let's put money on it. How about twenty grand if you win?"

I have to ask, "And what if I lose?"

"Then you don't show any of your pictures from the wedding, let the real wedding photographer sell his pictures, and let me into your room the night before we leave. I have a surprise for Nick Ferro, one he'll adore." Mandy's face is pinched into a snobby scowl. She comes from money. Her fake titties almost look real and I don't think that's her original nose either.

I shake my head and mutter, "Asshole."

"Oh, what's the matter? Too afraid to put your money where your mouth is? I hear that mouth has been everywhere else, so what's one more place?"

"Mandy!" Sophie scolds.

"Bitch," I bite back.

"Whore."

I roll my eyes and push up. "I don't have time for this shit. We can't all be pampered asses. I'll talk to you tomorrow

Soph." Just as I'm about to walk through the door, Mandy finishes whispering to her friends. "We'll double it. Come on Skylar, we know you're strapped for cash and if you're the best you have nothing to lose. Forty thousand bucks for the best shot of this wedding."

I pause in the doorway, unsure what to do. It's degrading, but it's enough to get me out of the mess I'm in. I can win without screwing with Nick. The lighting is a nightmare and he can't use his camera unless it's set on auto. His pictures will look like crap.

"They're using you. Walk away, Sky," Sophie whispers in my ear. These are her cousins. She can't stand Mandy, but the people you love and hate most are both invited to your wedding.

"Who picks the winner?" I ask and instantly hate myself for doing it, but I have to. There's no other way out of this.

Sophie closes her eyes and pinches the bridge of her nose. Mandy looks over at her cousin. "Sophie and Steven will pick, but you'll have to make it so they can't tell which picture belongs to which photographer. No cheating, trailer trash."

"Go fuck a cactus, classless cunt." Everyone gasps like they can't believe I really said those words. "Oh, shut up. It's not like you didn't know you were one. I'm just the only person brave enough to say it to your face."

Mandy grins wickedly, not denying my accusations. "So the bet is on?"

"Is she good for it?" I ask Sophie. My friend nods. After a moment, I nod and say, "Hell, yeah. I'm going to kick his ass so hard, even he won't find my shoe."

"You're so crude." Mandy's little nose crumples up before she goes to say more, but I'm already gone.

Beat Nick Ferro. I need the best shots. I already have one, but I don't know what shots he has. I tiptoe down the hall, into our room. After closing the door, I go over to his gear bag and fish out his only camera. Schmuck. I could break it and he'd be screwed, but I don't play like that.

Nick inhales and rolls away from me as I sneak the camera under my blankets to look at the illuminated screen. I flip through his shots and terror grabs hold of my throat. He's actually good. The angle of the portraits flatter everyone and his exposures are dead on. There's no way these were shot on auto. When I check his settings, I can see that they weren't. Damn it. Nick knows how to shoot.

As I press my eyes closed and silently curse, Nick yawns sleepily, "Taking dirty pictures with my camera? I'm a breast man. Make sure you get a good shot of underboob. I like that part." I gasp and try to conceal it, but it's too late. I'm totally busted. I drop the sheet and he can see me looking through his pictures. Nick is standing next to me, holding out his hand. "Hand it over."

I sigh and hold it up. "You're a liar."

"What?" He laughs.

"You said you couldn't shoot. You said you only shot on auto."

"I never said that."

"That's what you told my assistant when she interviewed you to second-shoot a wedding."

He laughs and climbs back into bed, leaving his camera next to him on the nightstand. "I knew who she was, Sky. I made shit up. Do you seriously not remember meeting me the first time?"

"I remember you moving in and making your studio look exactly like mine, you cocky ass."

He chortles. "Yeah, that was funny. But we met before that. I'm hurt Sky. I really am." Nick's teasing tone is getting to me, but I don't remember him. "Oh, come on—green hat, cord jacket, threadbare Chucks. I told you I wanted some pictures of a small wedding. You blew me off. I didn't even get a folder." He presses his hands mockingly to his bare chest and says the last few words like he's going to fake cry.

"I give everyone a folder."

"Except people you rule out. You ruled me out. I wasn't worthy of your services because of my secondhand clothing. Ironic, right? Ya know, since I'm filthy stinking rich and you're not." Nick winks at me before he lies back, tucks his hands behind his head, and settles into the mattress.

I slip down to my pallet on the floor and recall the instance he's telling me about. "You were wearing a John Deere hat."

Nick points his forefinger at me. "Bingo. And you blew me off."

I did toss him out pretty fast, but that wasn't why. There's no way in hell I'm telling him the truth, so I roll with it. "Yeah, I'm a snob. Total bitch." I pull up my blankets and roll away from him.

He's quiet for a moment and then softly says, "No, that's not it. I'll figure it out, Wendybird. And you should keep your kiss until you find the right guy. It's under your pillow."

My throat tightens as I reach underneath and find my thimble necklace. In Peter Pan, Wendy gave Peter the thimble and said it was a kiss. Nick knew. No one remembers that part of the story. My heart thumps and I don't know what to think of him. He shouldn't know these things, but he does. There's no way he's a Peter Pan freak like me. Yeah, guys get Peter Pan syndrome, but this isn't the same. His words choke me because they're filled with meaning beyond the gesture of handing back a trinket.

I've tried to find the right guy. The one previous time Mr. Right popped up, the situation was all wrong. There was already a ring on his finger and a woman on his arm. Sometimes that happens, and fate is too slow or we don't wait long enough. I thought that's what happened. After that first meeting with Nick, I was totally enthralled with him. I couldn't shoot his wedding because the magnetic pull was too strong and I liked him too much. His smile was so alluring—add in those blue eyes and I knew I'd be toast. The fastest way out of the wedding business is to flirt with the groom, so I threw him out without explanation. After all, it's not like I could tell him any of that. He'd already picked someone else.

Damn it. I'd wondered what happened to that guy, if he was happy. Now I know he's fine, because he's lying on the bed next to me, sound asleep.

CHAPTER 12

I toss and turn all night, devising ways to sabotage Nick. I can't play fair, not after seeing his pictures. Each photograph was well executed. His histograms were perfect—at least on the shots I had time to view. The next day, Sophie manages to keep Mandy away from me as we walk along the shoreline.

"You shouldn't have let her bait you like that." Concern fills her voice and her fingers twist her flowing ivory skirt. She's already dressed for dinner.

I shrug. "You have options. I don't."

She takes my arm and turns me toward her. My own dress swishes with the movement. We both stop walking. "Yes, you do. You can go home. Your parents can help you. Your mother has offered a million times."

I sigh dramatically, "Which is exactly why I can't close my shop and go crawling back to them. Sophie, I need to do this on my own. That bet with Mandy gives me a chance."

"Yeah, but you're going to have to do some things that aren't like you to ensure you win, aren't you? I mean, Nick doesn't suck, right? Otherwise, Mr. Stevens wouldn't have hired him."

I can't hold her gaze. "I am not ruining your wedding, don't worry, and I'm not going to break his gear." Hide it maybe, but not destroy it.

Sophie tilts her head at me and folds her arms over her chest. "You seriously expect me to believe that?"

I offer a half grin. "Enjoy your wedding and stop worrying about me. Come here for a second." I tug her hand and ask her to stand on a rock that's in the water. "Here, hand me your shoes."

Sophie doesn't want to do it. I can tell by her posture and the way she looks at the water. "Sky, the rock is slippery—I'll fall in and ruin my dress."

"They'd still be awesome pictures: a wet, white, wedding-ish looking dress. It'd fit right in with the boudoir shoot we're doing tomorrow night."

Sophie sighs, hands me her shoes, and pulls up the hem of her long dress. "I'm not doing that kind of shoot. I already told you I'm not comfortable with it."

"And I already told you that you can wear your wedding gown, lingerie, or whatever you want. The idea is to show off the sexy side of you."

Sophie snorts. "I don't have a sexy side."

"Yes you do. You just don't know it yet." I point. "Stand there and turn away from me, like you're considering swimming into the bay."

She laughs again as she turns. "With the mermaids?"

"You know that's why mermaids swim around topless all the time, right? It's because their boobs are too big and all bras are C shells." It's the worst joke I can think of, but it works.

Sophie looks over her shoulder at me and right before she makes a horrible face, I get the perfect shot. Her lips are parted and the worry line between her brows is gone. The setting sun highlights her hair and outlines her dress like it's made from moonbeams. It's perfect.

But she has no idea what I'm doing, so she looks appalled. "That is the worst joke I've ever heard. Like, ever."

"Well, D shells don't fit and that's why I can't swim away and be a mermaid." I sigh and look past her at the bay, wondering what life would be like if I didn't have to grow up and do this alone.

Sophie wades back to shore and puts her hand on my shoulder. "Come on, let's head to the rehcarsal before we're either late or you're abducted by mermaids with big boobs. Knowing you, you guys would form a club and I'd never see you again."

I burst out laughing and look down at my girls. "I don't think I'd make the cut."

"Don't be silly. You'd be their leader." Sophie and I walk back up to the house and just before we head down the road to the chapel, I tell her to go ahead. In a warning tone, she scolds, "Skylar."

Palms up, I back away. "I'm going to get my gear. Damn, Soph. You can't be suspicious of me the entire time. I only have my camera. I need my bags and reflectors and stuff. You know that."

"Fine, but leave Nick alone."

I smile broadly and my brows jut up, hiding beneath my bangs. "You like him." It took me a while to realize it, but she actually respects him. What the hell? "Sophie, he's the dick that's putting me out of business! How can you like him?"

"I don't like him!" She shushes me and leans in, grabbing my elbow conspiratorially as she does it. "I just think that something seems off. How can a guy so nice be such a jerk?"

"Uh, because he is a jerk?"

"Sky."

"Soph."

I make a noise in the back of my throat and pull away. "No, we're not doing this now. Go to the rehearsal. I'll be right behind you."

Sophie nods and walks off. The place we're staying has grounds with little paths that lead everywhere. Sophie's mother and father pass me on the front steps of the inn and hurry to catch up with her. I catch a glimpse of her dark eyes watching me slip inside. Thank God she left me. I'm not messing with his gear at all. I wouldn't do that. There just needs to be a little accident that looks like a mistake. I know exactly what to do.

CHAPTER 13

I already have my gear. I stashed it in the maid's closet down the hall from our room. I head there first to make sure everything is all right. I didn't trust leaving it in the room with Nick all day. He's in there now, getting ready. Earlier today, he followed Sophie around without telling me. The man was up at the crack of dawn and took some sunrise shots that I don't have. He didn't take a shower before he left, so he came back to the room about an hour ago to get ready for tonight.

I hoist my gear bag onto my shoulder, grab the little screwdriver, and head toward our door. I work each screw on the old knob until they're barely hanging on. When he grabs the knob, it'll come off in his hand leaving Nick stuck in our room. This hotel is really old, so it's the kind of thing that could happen. And no one is around at the moment to let him out. I hear him moving around in the bathroom and grin, pleased with myself.

After putting the screwdriver back in the maid's closet, I head to the rehearsal with a huge smile on my face. Just as I walk upon the group, I hear Mandy's voice behind me. "Trailer Trash." I don't turn, so she follows me. "You're going to lose this bet. Ask me how I know?" She's grinning like an evil fish.

"I'm not asking, Mandy. Go away," I snap at her. Turning, I see that they've already started. The minister is going over things with Sophie and her parents. My mother is sitting on the first row, while my father is standing in the far back corner. The bridesmaids are scattered, but close to Sophie. Everyone is here. Holy shit. Even Nick. I didn't see him at first. He was on his knee taking a shot. I don't see him until he rises, turns back and smiles at me.

My heart starts to pound as an uneasy feeling settles in my chest. If Nick is already here, who was in our room? I glance around and don't see who's missing until Sophie voices his name. "Where is Steven?"

His parents tell everyone he's running a little bit late. His mother adds, "There was an issue with his shower—there wasn't enough hot water—so Mr. Ferro allowed Steven to use his."

Half the bridesmaids swoon then and there, at the mere idea of Nick Ferro in a cold shower. We all look at him and picture his naked body, myself included. For a second, no one says anything, until Nick adds, "It was the least I could do. If it was my wedding, I hope someone would do the same." He winks at me. The fucker. He knew I was going to mess with him.

My lips part and people turn to see who Nick is looking at. I try to say something, but can't. A moment later, Sophie's cell vibrates. She pulls it out and presses it to her ear. Super suck. "What? Okay, don't worry about it. We'll just do it later than we thought." Sophie throws an evil glare my way before she hangs up. A false, calm smile resumes, spreading from one cheek to the other. "Well, he was on his way when something went wrong. The doorknob came off in his hand and he's locked in Nick and Sky's room. Hotel Maintenance said they'd have the door open in about ten minutes or so."

Sophie's mom presses her fingers to her lips. "Oh, but we'll be late for dinner."

Mandy grins like the Jersey devil. "No prob. I'll fix it." She smacks her gum and calls someone. People start talking and the last thing I hear is her annoyed snapping voice, "Well, then, I'll double it. Just fix it, or it'll be in all the society papers and not in a good way." Mandy sighs way too loud when she hangs up. It's as if she were lifting weights. She smiles this huge fake smile and says, "Well, that's taken care of, we can be as late as we want. I'll call over when Steven arrives and they'll just reschedule everything. I had to book the room for a few extra hours, but anything for my cousin."

"Oh, thank you, Mandy!" Sophie's mom hugs the girl and the two of them disappear at the front, talking.

Nick makes his way back to me, subtly, with his camera hiding half his face. He's grinning. "So, that didn't go as planned, did it?"

CHAPTER 14

I lift my camera and take a shot. It sucks. The light is flat and there's nothing interesting going on. "I haven't any idea what you mean."

He laughs. "Uh huh. Next time don't stash your gear right before you plan an attack. It'll be less noticeable."

I gape, turning to him. "You found it?"

"I had to grab Steven another towel, and imagine my surprise when I saw all your gear on the closet floor." He grins at me, stepping closer, closing the space between us. That gorgeous face becomes one hundred percent serious. "You don't want to mess with me. You're a lightweight with this kind of stuff."

"How would you know?"

"Hello? I'm putting you out of business."

My jaw drops. "So you admit it?"

"Of course I admit it." Nick's camera is pressed to his face taking another shot. When he looks over at me, something flashes in his eyes. It's as if he doesn't want to do it, but will destroy everything I've made. I'll have to go crawling back to my parents by the time he's through with me. I won't even have a penny.

I nod slowly. "So this whole time, you've been gunning for me."

"Of course. You can't have two studios that close together. It's ridiculous." He starts to walk away and I follow.

"Why me?" I mean it. I ask the question to his back and instantly hate myself for doing it. It makes me sound weak and whiny. I swallow hard, letting anger flow through my veins and wishing I could make my fingertips fire bolts straight at his face.

Nick turns around and answers. "Because you were the best."

"I still am."

Nick offers that sexy half-crooked Ferro smirk before leaning in close and whispering in my ear. "No, you're not— not anymore." He walks away without another word. All my suspicions were true. Amy thought I was crazy, but I wasn't. The guy did everything on purpose. He did everything from stealing clients to spreading rumors about me.

I want to bury him. Before I consider what I'm about to do, I blurt out, "Care to make a wager on that?"

Nick stops in his tracks. He looks over his shoulder at me. "Please, how much more juvenile can you get?"

"Quite a bit, actually. But there's already a bet going on, so this would just be a side bet anyway."

Steven is walking toward us, so I explain quickly about the bet for determining the better photographer. I tell him Sophie's cousins have a lot of money and are bored. I don't tell him the bet is with me. "I already know I can kick your ass. It's just a matter of time and the rest of them will notice."

He laughs. "A little cocky, aren't we?"

"Me? You're the arrogant bastard who told Mrs. Getty that I forgot my meds, but I'm nice when I'm on them." I use air quotes for the last few words along with a deeper, doofy voice that's meant to sound like Nick.

His laugh grows louder as he tries not to smile. Nick looks up the road, then back at me. "And what are the terms of this bet? Because the way I figure it, after this wedding, you're washed up anyway."

Ouch. "Yeah, unless people buy my stuff, which they will. And one term of the first bet will make it so they can't buy your pictures, only mine when I win. So how about this—when I win, you close your store and jump off a bridge—gear and all." I beam at him, smiling up into his masculine face.

He's really nice to look at, like seriously nice. Taunting him is one of my favorite things to do. I realize it as I'm standing here, wishing I were taller, so we could be nose-to-nose. I want to laugh in his face and show him up in every way possible. Note to self: wear heels tomorrow.

Nick laughs my comment away, shaking his head. "Like that'll ever happen. There is nothing you could bet that would tempt me in the slightest."

"No? Are you sure?" I circle him once, my eyes sweeping over his body before stopping in front of his face. "Nothing at all?" Holy shit, his smile is beautiful. It glows so brightly I'm no longer sure what he thinks I offered him.

Nick can't help it, his gaze dips to the ground and then up to his camera. When he turns away he says dryly, "You're betting your body against my business? You must think pretty highly of yourself."

I gasp, not realizing that's what it sounded like. Leaning in, I punch his arm quickly. As Steven walks past us, I say hurriedly, "No! I'll close my shop and be your model. It's dually degrading. You wanted a topless model wearing next-to-nothing. I heard you were having a hard time finding someone. That's what I'm offering you perv—a double slam, not to be slammed."

Stroking his chin with his hand, his mouth opens. I have no idea what he's going to say. What I'm offering is humiliating enough that I expect him to take the bet, especially if he's that confident that he'll win.

But he says, "Tempt me more, Sky. Offer one more thing and I'll say yes." Those sapphire eyes bore into me until my stomach is twisting in knots. I can't look away and I have no idea what he's thinking, but I can tell the nature of his thoughts. No guy looks at a girl like that and is picturing something of a friendly nature. Nah, Nick has me stripped naked and doing something.

"What?" I ask, because I can't believe he really means it. I need him to take this bet. The pieces of the messed up puzzle of my life are falling into place. If I win, he's gone. I can take the money from slutty bridesmaid and I can expand. It'll make sure my store has more than a toehold. My career will be set in stone. I won't have to beg my parents for money or say I was wrong. This is beyond perfect, depending on this last part.

Nick's dark brows lift and he gives me a look that makes me shiver. Leaning in close to my ear, he whispers, "You close your doors and be the model on my logo forever, and—since I'll get those parts of the bet anyway..."

"You mean you're trying," I interrupt.

He reaches out quickly and grabs my lower lip between his fingers, effectively silencing me. "I'm not trying. I'm succeeding. There's about a snowball's chance in hell that you'll win. My final term, though, the one that makes or breaks this bet—open your legs for me for one night. That's worth this wager. Think about it." He drops my lip and steps away from me, leaving me breathless, my heart flopping down into my shoes.

That would suck beyond measure. There'd be nothing more humiliating, or degrading. I'm practically selling myself to this guy. He's not the novice I thought he was when I made the bet with Mandy. He's also not as unassuming as everyone else believed. Nick Ferro is cold and cunning. I'd bet anything that handing me the thimble back last night was a way to play with my brain, so I'd second guess myself. Well, I'm not going to. I am the best and I know I can shoot better than he can.

With every ounce of determination I can muster, I grab his shoulder and spin him around. Grabbing his tie forcefully, I pull his face down to mine. "I don't need time to think about it. I know I can kick your ass any day of the week and twice on Sunday. Get ready to bend over Nick. You have a wager." I toss his tie in his face before offering my hand to him. Nick grins, takes it, and shakes my hand hard, sealing our deal.

Still holding my hand, he pulls me to him in a swift movement. "No backing out." The yank startles me and lands my chest firmly against his. He does it on purpose, knowing it'll throw me off balance. There's an attraction between us. We both feel it, we both recognize it, but that's all it is and nothing more. I'm not that dumb girl who falls for a Ferro.

My grip on his hand tightens and I push into him harder. "Sky Thompson doesn't run. And you better pick which bridge you'll be jumping from. I was serious about that part." I step back and wink at him—the way he's been winking at me—and turn on my heel. As I walk away I can feel his hot gaze slip over my back and down to my hips.

Look all you want, Nick. You're not going to win.

CHAPTER 15

The rehearsal is basically a dry run of the wedding. The coordinator isn't too annoying. She's actually very helpful, otherwise I'd get stuck doing her job. It's not until Sophie is on her dad's arm, ready to walk down the aisle, that I notice Nick and I want the same space.

I bump his shoulder and push him into a pew. "Move, Ferro. You're blocking my shot." Missing the prized picture of the bride coming down the aisle is an unforgivable offense. Apparently, Nick has a decent eye because he made a beeline for this location at the same time as me. He didn't follow or look around—

Nick knew where he wanted to be for that shot.

Nick shoulders me back and I practically step on Sophie as she passes. Sophie smiles and gives me a deadly look that says she will kill me if I trip her on her wedding day. Nick pushes his hair away from his eyes. It's warm and his dark hair is damp and sticking to his skin along with his dress shirt. The sudden thought of sliding my slippery body against his flashes through my mind; I chase it away with a mental broom. Thoughts like that are poisonous, but they keep popping up. The way he moves, something in the depths of his eyes, that arrogant smirk—it just makes me think it's a mask. The man I'm seeing behind that is the real Nick. This is, well, it's a façade and there's nothing I'd like to do more than tear it away and see the mess beneath. I can relate to an honest mess—perfection, not so much.

Speaking of which, my mother takes this moment to publically scold me. "Skylar, let the professional take this shot. You're in his way." Mom is sitting on a pew right in front of me. I suck in a breath and try to steady myself.

Nick's gaze flicks to the side and takes in my reaction. Great. Now he has more ammo. Launch my Mom on me, turn me batshit crazy, and I'll mess up. That's the biggest chink in my armor and he sees it like sunlight on a bear's bottom. I change my expression and laugh, like she's joking, but Nick's already seen. So has everyone else. Good old Mom just changed everyone's opinion of me in a few seconds.

Nick grabs my elbow. I look up at him, suspicious. "This isn't the only spot we both want. There are three more, at least. Let's flip for them."

I nod, because it seems like the fairest, fastest thing to do.

"Aisle shot. Ready?" I nod. "Heads or tails?"

"Heads," I answer as Nick fishes a coin from his pocket. The rest of the wedding planning continues around us. We back into a corner, half listening, while we sort out who gets which spot.

Nick flips the coin, catches it in his palm, and then flips it over onto the back of his hand. "Sorry, it's tails. I get the aisle." I don't say anything. Nick holds the coin and says, "Ring shot, we both want the front center aisle, right?" I nod. "Call it in the air."

"Heads." I always say heads.

Nick catches it, flips the coin over, and my stomach sinks. "That's two for me. And there's one last shot that I'm sure we both want the same shooting location."

"The kiss." The kiss at the end of the ceremony is everything. It's the picture the couple hangs over their mantle for the next million years.

Nick nods and flips the coin. "Call it."

I stick with my previous choice. "Heads."

Nick catches and flips the coin. My stomach sinks. "Wow, you have really bad luck. What are the odds of losing all three?"

I roll my eyes, not wanting to answer before I walk away but I can't help myself. "It won't matter where I stand. I'll still get a better shot than you." Well, that's what I say out loud, my face serene and my smile placid. Inside my head, I'm screaming, throwing a tantrum like a two-year-old, but with more expletives.

Nick uses a smooth voice. "I like this side of you." I don't look back at him and instead keep my eyes focused on Sophie. "I hope it's there when you lose. That confidence borders on defiance. I already have plans for us and that'll make it all the more pleasant. See you around, Wendybird."

When I turn to look back at him, Nick has his arms folded over his chest and a single brow raised. He smirks at me, like he knows he's already won. "Don't call me that." I shoot him the bird and keep walking.

My mother gasps, horrified, as I pass her, but only one voice is laughing.

CHAPTER 16

Deegan falls into step beside me. "Wow. You guys get along great." He's clean and looks nice in his suit, but like everyone else, he's got a brow beaded with sweat. The night air is thick and soupy. It's the kind of humidity that you can almost see.

I stare at the ground as I walk in swift, determined strides. "Yeah, that's the asshole who's trying to put me out of business. We just tossed a coin for the key locations to shoot from during the wedding and I lost all three times." Figures. I have horrible luck. Part of me says it doesn't matter, that I'm a creative genius (or lunatic depending on who you talk to), but my point is that I will find a better spot, a better shot. Losing the coin tosses won't screw me. I ignore the sinking feeling in the pit of my stomach that insists I'm totally screwed.

Deegan's brows lift as his mouth gapes. He looks like a grouper or an orange roughy. Actually, I've never seen that fish, except on the menu at Red Lobster. Damn, I'm hungry. I glance at Deegan and notice how yummy he looks. The glance doesn't go unnoticed.

Deegan grins and gives me a sweet smile. "Well, maybe I can help you take your mind off both the Sith Lord and your camera-wielding nemesis after dinner. Sophie mentioned you know the island pretty well and that there's a mermaid cove not far from here."

I laugh and try to hide my blush by turning away and making my hair fall forward. I press my camera to my face and snap a picture, mostly to hide my embarrassment. When we were little, we pretended we were mermaids and nicknamed the spot mermaid cove. "She told you about the cove, huh?"

"Yup, sure did." Deegan places his hands behind his back and walks next to me.

"Did she mention that mermaids wear clothes and only appear for girls?"

"I'm down with that." He lifts his palms up like he means no harm. "It'd still be fun to see with the right person. Between the Imperial March and the shower curtain rumors, I think you're the right person."

My face flames redder. "Oh God, you heard about that, too?" At least he didn't add 'crotch grabber' to the list.

"Saw it." I make a noise and try to walk away, but he takes me by the elbow and turns me toward him. "Have you ever heard the expression, imperfectly perfect? Well, that's you." Deegan offers a shy smile.

My stomach twists so hard I can't look at him. This feels like high school and he's my first crush. What happened to the confident woman who offered to castrate Nick Ferro? Tucking my hair behind my ear, I nod. I look up at him from under my lashes, not meaning to do it, but it happens anyway, "You made that expression up, but yes to the walk anyway."

"Okay, Mermaid. See you after dinner." Deegan returns to the wedding party and resumes his place by Steven. Nick watches us speaking, but keeps his distance. There's possessiveness in Nick's eyes that surprises me. I'm not his. I can talk to anyone I like. I could sleep with Deegan and Nick can't stop me. Maybe I should be the slutty bridesmaid for once and have a fling with Deegan. God knows I brought enough sexy panties.

CHAPTER 17

The moonlight is stunning. It dances across the dark water. Deegan and I sit hip-to-hip in the darkness, perched on the edge of a large rock that is submerged in the sand and extends out into the water. Our shoes are behind us. We walked barefoot to the edge and put our feet in. It conjures memories of the other night with Nick.

Deegan is safer, more normal. The Ferros aren't average and their family is constantly involved in some scandal or another. I don't want that life. I don't want him. Even as the words form in my mind, I feel the lie and it's growing. I have a thing for Nick. I know I do. I'm hoping that this beautiful young man sitting next to me can shatter my infatuation. Deegan is real and has been from the start. He's also not some pampered ass, either, so I respect him more than Nick.

Stop thinking about Nick! I mentally scold myself. I remind myself that I'm sitting next to a hot guy, with a very nice package in those pants. Not that I usually think like that, but it's hard to ignore it now.

I lift my foot from the water and stretch my tired toes. It makes ripples that fan out from the rock and into the dark water.

Until now, Deegan has been making pleasantries. I laugh, he talks, and so on. It's nice. So when he mentions Ferro, it throws me for a loop. "Uh, Sky, it's not that I don't trust your roommate or anything, but check the coins." Deegan is looking out at the water when he says it, his gaze fixated on some point far in the distance. "I bet he dumps his change on the dresser at the end of the day."

I smile, thinking he's joking. "Why should I do that?" The side of his face is striking. He has a five o'clock shadow I imagine feeling rough under my palms. His tie is off, behind us somewhere with his jacket and shoes. The collar of that pristine pale purple shirt is open and I can see a tiny bit of his chest below.

"He won all three spots." He looks at me and cocks his head to the side. "Make sure he was playing fair. It wouldn't surprise me if he had a double-sided coin in his pocket. The man is a Ferro. Don't put anything past him. They all play to win and like to screw with anyone who gets in the way." Deegan's face scrunches up as he glances away. "Well, maybe not screw you, but you get the idea. I don't like the idea of him messing around with you like that."

For a second, I wonder if Deegan overheard our bet. I shove the thought aside. "I don't think Nick is that devious, but I'll check. If he is, he's going to wish he never met me."

Deegan chuckles softly. When he turns his face to mine, we're a breath apart. My heart pounds harder and I forget to breathe. My eyes drift to his lips and I think about it. I could be the slutty bridesmaid, just this once. No one is out here. We're practically on the other side of the island, which is mostly a nature preserve, and shrouded in darkness. He could slip the strap of my dress off my shoulder and run his palm over my bare skin. I could lie back on the cold rock and let his body warm me inside and out. Those beautiful hands could feel every inch of me. I could let him. I could.

Deegan's eyes drift to my lips before darting back to my eyes. He repeats the same movement several times leaning closer to me ever so slowly. The rush of breath I'd lost comes back and I can't hide that I've been imagining our tangled naked bodies. My face grows hot as my body pulses in all the right places. I want this kiss. I want his lips on mine. Just for now, I want him to make me forget all my problems—to forget who I am. He can see it in my eyes.

Deegan's lips brush against mine, making my skin prickle. I lean in closer, threading my fingers through his hair. The kiss is tame at first, but shifts quickly. Neither of us speaks. It's like he knew this was coming, even if I didn't. I don't do things like this. I'm no exhibitionist, no one-night stand chick aching for another lay. That's not me. But it doesn't matter because here I am, falling back and pulling this stranger down with me. His firm body eagerly follows and presses my back into the cold, wet stone.

Slow down, a voice in my mind warns, but I ignore it.

No! For once, I want things to go my way and I throw caution to the wind. I've been nothing but cautious and look where it's gotten me. I'm going to win this bet or go groveling back to my parents. And if I lose, I offered up myself as the prize. What the hell is wrong with me? Why'd I do that? Hindsight is always crystal clear, but at that moment it seemed like a logical move.

Stop thinking. I want to be a siren and this is my cove. I want to seduce this man for no reason other than I want to and I can. When I was a teenager, I'd thought about mythological mermaids to the point it was scandalous. I never mentioned it to Amy. I can't imagine the conversations that would ensue.

This isn't like you, slow down.

No, this is me. I have Deegan here alone. He wants me, here and now. I can feel it and I'm not going to stop him. Deegan's hands are all over my skin, gripping, cupping, and feeling my curves through my clothes. One hand slips under the hem of my dress and I'm in heaven. As I come up from a passionate kiss, Deegan works his way down my neck. Eyes closed, I gasp for air. He presses our hips firmly together and rocks our bodies with the rhythm of the dark waters, filling me with naughty thoughts.

I moan and smile serenely for a moment, thinking about how strange this is for me, but loving it all the same. It's been too long since I've been with a guy. I work eighty hours a week and have no life. There's no time to meet anyone and no time to do anything even remotely like this. As it is, I have to be up at the hotel to take Sophie's boudoir pictures later.

I'm always working. There's never any time for fun and it kills me that all that work was all for nothing.

Don't give up yet, a voice whispers in the back of my mind, as Deegan teases me ruthlessly with kisses.

I won't. I'm a fighter and I'm not going to roll over and die. Nick Ferro is going to have to shove me headfirst into the ground before I stop trying to win.

Nick Ferro. Nick. The name echoes through my thoughts, but my mind becomes filled with a lust-ridden fog that makes me unable to think. I blink slowly, enjoying the way Deegan's hot mouth feels on my skin as I stare at the stars.

My life hasn't turned out the way I wanted. I follow the rules, playing fairly in every way, but always come out behind. I'm breaking the rules this time. I'm going to do this with Deegan and not care about the consequences.

Deegan whispers in my ear, "Tell me what you want."

"You. Now." I manage to reply, but my voice is all air. Reaching for him, I tug his shirt out from his slacks and run my palms up his back before digging my nails in. Each one bites his skin as I scratch and pull him toward me.

Deegan grins and goes for my neck again, this time undressing me as the kisses spread lower and lower. He places the garments under my back as he removes each one so my hot skin isn't on the cold stone. Then he dips his head, and oh, my God!

My eyes close as I savor the sensation of not having a worry in the world. In the very back of my mind, in the places where I think dark thoughts live, some part of me can still realize that I'm using Deegan to forget everything, even if it's only temporary.

It's worth it. Isn't it? I mean, it's not like I'm a slut. I've only slept with one guy before. It was a long time ago and we were in a serious relationship. Yes, it was in high school, but that's the last relationship I had. Our relationship fell apart when he left for college and some blond co-ed mistakenly fell on his dick. I walked in on them. That's pathetic. That event was my last sexual encounter.

Stop thinking!

Deegan's breathless voice pulls me back. "Are you sure?" He kisses way below my neckline and then hovers there, waiting for an answer.

"Do you have a condom?" He nods and the black square appears out of thin air. He holds it between two fingers and looks down at me. His chest is toned and his abs are lean. Coupled with the trim waist, he's my type to the core. I nod and pull him toward me, making his lips meet mine.

My heart pounds harder and faster as the kiss grows hotter and hotter. Deegan's fingers are in my hair, tangling it and pushing it out of my face as he rocks his hips against mine. I'm only wearing panties and Deegan's down to a pair of black tighty-whities. What do you call those? I know the only barrier keeping him from me is the thin layer of fabric between us. He's obviously ready, and every time he moves against me, I want this even more.

Just as I gasp again, about to beg him to do all sorts of naughty things to me, my eyelids flutter open. The shore behind us is dark, but I can make out hazy outlines in the moonlight. Rocks of different sizes litter the shore as far as the eye can see. I blink slowly and my eyes focus on a shape that's too soft to be made of stone. A dark outline is standing on the shore, leaning against a dead tree—watching.

Sucking in air, I grip Deegan's wrist hard, stopping him. "Someone's there."

"No, can't be." The condom is open and the wrapper is gone. Did he toss it into the water? I'm not a hippie, but I don't toss trash on the ground—or in the water. He's slipped his bottoms off and is in the process of hooking a finger around my panties.

I squirm so he can't pull them off. "Deegan, we can't do this—someone's watching." The words come out in a rush.

Deegan looks down at me and smiles like I'm a child. "If you wanted to stop, you should have said so."

"I didn't. I mean I do want you, but I'm not doing it with someone watching." Our eyes are locked and mine are pleading for him to turn around and look.

Deegan sighs loudly, like he's massively annoyed and turns around. The way he scans the shore says everything—he thinks I'm making this up—until he flinches, spying the voyeur.

The man in the shadows finally speaks as he steps toward us. "That was incredibly fast. Sorry Sky."

Deegan's face pinches in anger and he moves like he's going to slug the guy, but I don't give him the chance.

Fury boils inside of me as I cover my breasts with my hands and try to find my clothes. "Nick! What the hell is wrong with you? Why are you watching us, you perv?" I'm shrieking and shaking.

Deegan sits on the rock, naked and stares at Nick. "You're an asshole, man."

"Likewise." Nick walks over to the edge of the boulder with that confident swagger of his and redirects his comments at me. "Sophie wants you. She said she was tired and wanted to do the boudoir shoot now, which was about an hour ago. I told you I wouldn't shoot without you, so I waited."

I try to grab my bra, but I'm trembling so much that it falls into the water. Black water pours through the holes in the pink lace, making it sink. I stare at it for a second before lifting my gaze to Nick. "You!" I have no words. I growl like a lunatic and pull on my dress. He's seen me naked twice! Twice!

As I get to my feet, Deegan takes my hand and touches me gently. The caress sends a shiver up my spine. I nearly melt right then and there. It was the perfect touch. "I'll be there for you anytime."

I offer him a nod and mouth, *sorry*.

CHAPTER 18

When I get to the shore, I shove Nick as hard as I can. "Why were you watching? What the hell is wrong with you?"

Nick laughs. "Everyone would have watched that."

I don't like the way he said the last word. "Excuse me?" We're far enough from Deegan, but not close enough to the hotel for anyone to hear us. I shout at him, "No, they wouldn't have. They would have kept on walking."

Nick's dimple appears as he smiles. Bastard. "You're so cute when you're mad, but you're wrong, babe, and I'll tell you why. Any person who heard the noises you were making would have stopped and stared because you were so loud it was impossible to ignore."

"I was not!"

He shrugs his shoulders like it doesn't matter. "Yes, you were and seeing a woman in the throes of passion and behaving so uninhibited, well, fuck Sky— anyone would look and stare..." His eyes drift over me before he adds, "and want you for himself."

A rush of anger bursts through me. I pull my arm back and swing, but the punch doesn't connect. Nick catches my fist and then gets into my face. In that sultry voice of his, he breathes, "Why are you trying to punch me? I'm telling you the truth. I'd just found you and was shocked. Did you want me to leave and go shoot Sophie's photos without you?"

He's still holding my fist. "No."

I try to yank my fist away but his grip tightens. Nick leans in closer and those dark lashes dip to my lips. "I wonder." He doesn't finish his thought, which drives me nuts.

As I continue to try to pull away, he manages to hold on without hurting me. "I don't care what you wonder. Let me go and if you tell anyone you saw me with Deegan—"

Nick releases me and steps back, chortling before walking away. "Called it!" He raises his fist in the air and whoops like he won something.

I remain behind him, perplexed. "You called what?"

"I knew you were the slutty bridesmaid. Hey, when we do it, I'd prefer some place less slimy." Nick hastens his pace, making it difficult for me to keep up with him even though I'm practically running. I lose sight of him somewhere between the hotel and the road.

CHAPTER 19

When the big white hotel comes into view, it's glowing golden against the night sky. I stop for a second and take in the view. I loved this place so much and now it's tarnished with these horrible memories.

When I get to the house, there's no sight of Nick. I smooth my hair and head to the elevator, very self-conscious of my free-swinging state and the sheer fabric of my dress. Mr. Stevens walks up beside me and presses the up button. "It's so good to see you again, Skylar." He fumbles my name when he finally takes a good look at me. My hair is a mess, I'm flushed, and

I'm pretty sure my high beams are on and very visible.

I stare straight ahead and act like nothing is abnormal. "Thank you. It's nice to see you, too."

The elevator door opens and a few guys from the wedding party walk out. Their eyes dart straight to my nipples. They smirk like they know what I was doing and would be happy to do me again. One winks as he passes, but makes certain no one else can see. He acts like he's holding the elevator door for me, but leans in and whispers, "Room 207."

I don't respond. Mr. Stevens can't avoid the cramped space without making it look as if he doesn't want to be near me. So instead of excusing himself, or answering a non-existent call, he steps into the box with me and presses the number for his floor. The old guy stares straight ahead, only asking, "Which floor?" I tell him and he punches the button.

The doors close and silence ensues. There is no music to cover my horror or to make the ride seem shorter. We both stare straight ahead, refusing to acknowledge that anything is amiss.

Finally, Mr. Stevens says, "Nice weather we're having."

I nod way too much and practically throw myself through the doors when they open. "Yes, have a good night." I say over my shoulder as I exit. Then I make a horrible mistake. When he starts to talk, I stop and turn toward him.

The older man fumbles his words and looks everywhere but at me. His hands are gripped tightly as his gaze darts all over the place. "Well, you too. Well, I mean, have a fun, uh," he stares straight at me with a deer in the headlights look, "well, have a nice night. Be good." The doors slip shut and save us from further agony.

I'm never going to be able to talk to Sophie's father-in-law again, ever. Holidays are going to suck. He's going to be like, remember the time I saw your breasts, but I didn't look? And I'm going to be like yeah, Mr. Stevens, those were good times.

Someone shoot me. Please. This can't get worse, it just can't.

When I arrive at our room out of breath, Nick looks up from the bed, where he's grabbing his gear. The man straightens and tilts his head to the side and tut-tuts me. "Sky, you can't bang the entire groomsmen party. Well, at least not all on the same night. Save some for tomorrow. Damn, woman."

I snap. I mean, it's not like I can take a lot of teasing to start with, but I usually maintain my composure. I can't stand it when people get the better of me and I never ever show it, but something about Nick makes me crazy. I do idiotic things when he's around and so I act on my feelings by raising my hands over my head and charging him while growling so low it sounds like there's a bear living in my stomach.

I launch myself at him, my hands aiming for his neck. I bounce across the bed like a Gummy Bear and knock the man to the floor. Nick doesn't think I'll do it, he expects me to stop, but I don't. I plow right into him and down he goes, shocked expression and all. Straddling him I take my pointer finger and jab it to the tip of his nose, pressing up until it can't move another inch.

That's when I hiss, "If you do one more thing, just one more thing, I swear to God I'll rip your lungs out of your body through your nose!"

For a second he says nothing. The expression on his face doesn't change, he just watches me with those cool blue eyes. My anger settles and it's like he senses it. Nick reaches for my wrist and pulls my hand away. Our eyes are locked the entire time and my heart won't slow down. It thumps and races until I'm deaf. I don't know how much time passes like that, but I feel myself being drawn to him. It's like there's a line there, one that no one can see, tugging me to his chest—to his lips.

I want his arms to wrap around me and never let go. We gaze at each other much too long, before I break it and look down at his hand on my wrist. Deegan's touch felt nice, but Nick's is incomparable. His grip is firm, so I know he's strong, but there's a softness in the way he holds me that is unlike Deegan. It's unlike anyone who's ever held me. Nick watches me as my gaze dips to his hand. A second later he releases me. I don't move. I meant to beat him up, I really did, but now I can't.

Insults are swirling in my mind, but that's not what comes out of my mouth. "You really would have watched?" Nick is so still, like a gazelle that knows it's been spotted by a lion. Is he that kind of guy? It shouldn't matter to me, but for some reason it does. I want him to say no. I want him to be the man I see under all the polish and charm. That guy wouldn't watch.

"It's difficult *not* to watch you." His gaze darts away from mine, making my heart beat harder. "I admit I handled it wrong. I didn't mean to invade your private life like that. I'm sorry. It won't happen again." Nick takes my arms and shifts so that I'm sitting on the floor and not straddling his legs.

My jaw is hanging open. He likes me? I blurt out the words before I can stop myself, "I don't understand."

Nick looks at me out of the corner of his eye as he reaches for his camera. While placing the strap around his neck, he replies, "You don't understand what?"

"Why? Why are you putting me out of business?" I get to my feet and walk over to him, but he won't look at me. He fumbles the lens cap and it drops to the floor. The piece of plastic rolls under the bed and we both go to grab it at the same time. Our fingers brush, inciting a warm surge of something unknown to flow through me. His touch is electric; it's pure energy, addictive and warm.

I pick up the cap and hold it out for him. He looks at it and that smirk returns. Game over. I'm not going to get another piece of truth from those lips tonight. When he starts to speak, I press my finger to his lips and say, "Don't. You're better than that. And by the way, if you tell anyone that I jumped at you like a rabid rabbit, I'll deny it." My mask is up and my smile is hiding every feeling I have. I grab my gear bag and I turn toward the door, but I pause as I feel his fingers wrap around my wrist one by one. I look back at him.

His smile falters and fades. "Don't."

Something is different than it was before. My gear bag slips off my shoulder as Nick reaches for my chin. He gently slides a finger beneath it and lifts my face toward his, eyes watching my mouth as he does it. I can barely breathe. My heart pounds violently and I shiver at his touch. Parts of me awaken and respond, parts I didn't know were there. The pull between us is intense, unstoppable. It's ensnared both of us and with each second, our lips move closer and closer. Images of bare, slick skin enter my mind. I picture our bodies tangled together. My breath catches in my throat and the distance between us closes.

Just as his beautiful, full lips brush against mine, a phone chirps. The spell breaks and we dart apart.

Nick runs his hand over the back of his neck, unable to look at me. "See you down there." He opens the door and walks out.

"Yeah," I answer without looking at him or asking for an explanation of where 'down there' is exactly. I pace the floor, trying to breathe and holding onto my heart. It's ready to jump if he snaps his fingers. Oh God, I want him to snap his fingers. I almost want to lose the bet just so I can be with him.

I stare at the wall until I come down from my lusty high and then put on clean clothes from my suitcase. After I'm respectably dressed again, I bend down, grab my gear bag, reach for the doorknob and twist—it comes off in my hand.

CHAPTER 20

I drop my bag and scream at the top of my lungs. "Get back here you son of a bitch!" But there's no answer. Nick is long gone. I turn, pressing my back to the door and slide down until my butt hits the carpet. Clawing at my temples, I tug on my hair, wondering how I let him do this to me. It was the dumbest payback ever, but I didn't see it coming. Who pulls a prank like that? It's a reprank. Bastard.

I push up and glance around the room, noticing the subtle difference for the first time—no phone. The antique looking brass phone is missing from the desk. I can't call down for help. The thought makes me lunge for my bag. I didn't have my cell phone earlier, it's with my gear. I unfasten the straps and dig through. No phone.

"I'm going to kill him. I am. How did he even get Sophie to agree to let him be at the shoot?" I glance around, not knowing what to do. If I figure out how to bust the door down, the hotel is going to make me pay for it. Not that there's an ax in here or something.

I sit down hard on the bed and let out a rush of air. Should I stay here and let him have this shoot? What if he's lying? I mean, Sophie said the shoot was later, not now. She wanted to wait until her hideous cousins were asleep. But if she didn't want to do the sexy session now, why else would Nick lock me in the room? I think and think, but there's no answer. Nothing drifts to the top of my mind and it's so frustrating.

I have to find him. I push off the bed and go to the only way out of the room— the window. I'm on the third floor. A fall from that height won't kill a person, right? I pull up the window and lean on the sash.

There's no screen. Screens would look unsightly on the hotel façade. Then again, so would a twenty-something white girl hanging out the window. If I hang my legs over the ledge, I can lower myself down to the next floor. The roof of porch is directly below my window. I could knock on the window of the room below me and ask them to let me in.

It's absurd, but it's also my only idea. I grab my camera and take only one lens. After attaching it to the body, I swing it around my neck and drape the heavy thing down my back. The contraption is so heavy it feels like it's going to strangle me. I sit on the window sash and swing one leg over. The pit of my stomach dips when I look out. The ground is so far away, and the gardens are filled with spiky things, like old pointy pieces of iron fence and roses. If I fall, I'll be impaled and showered in rose petals.

With my heart slamming into my ribs, I swing the other foot over, twist and go for it. Slowly, I lower myself until I'm hanging from the windowsill, my camera dangling from my back. My shoes sweep the air looking for a foothold, but there is none. It's farther than I'd thought. Damn it. What am I going to do? I try to do a pull-up and go back into the room. As I pull, a grunting noise comes from deep inside my chest, but no matter how hard I try, I just hang there.

"Daddy, look!" a little girl's voice calls out below. "There's a lady falling out of a window!"

Shit! I can't look over my shoulder, but I feel her eyes on me.

A male voice sounds annoyed at first and then panicked. "Danielle, stop making up—oh my God! Go inside and tell them to call the fire department. Go quickly."

CHAPTER 21

I don't know what to do. If I admit I put myself here…oh God. So I swallow any pride I have left and say it. "Help!"

The guy below sounds freaked out. "Don't worry. Hold on, someone will get you. What room are you in? I'll come and pull you in."

"The door is broken." I call it down to him as I feel my fingers begin to slip.

The guy yells and suddenly everyone and their mother is outside. My mother comes, too. "Get down this instant! You're making a spectacle of yourself!" Good old mom, always thinking of my wellbeing.

"I would if I could, Ma!" I yelp as my fingers slip. My palms are sweating and sliding. I'm losing my grip. The people below gasp and I hear a siren approaching. Someone is banging on my door, but it doesn't open. They must see the knob is broken, because they suddenly stop. "How far is the ledge?"

"Don't be stupid, Skylar. You'll break your neck. Just wait for a professional to get you down. I can see the truck now." Mom replies quickly.

I can't see anything. The hotel staff has a ladder, but it's too short. It only goes up to the second floor. There's a guy on the ladder, a few feet from me. "We should have stayed in the cove."

"Deegan?"

"Don't jump, Sky. It's too far. The ladder truck is almost here. Hold on."

"I can't!" My hands have slipped so that only my fingers are holding me up.

"I can't reach you from here, Sky. Don't you dare let go. They're almost here. Hang on."

I feel so stupid. The crowd below has grown larger and everyone is watching me. My hands continue to slide over the window sill. I can't stop them.

The ladder truck below is calling to me and I'm trying to dig my nails into the plaster. "I'm going to fall!" One hand slips completely free and swings through the air. I scream and the other hand follows. My ass hits the roof hard and gravity pulls me down faster than I thought possible, directly toward Deegan. I'm yelling and I cannot stop.

"Sky!" Deegan looks down, but before he has a chance to move, I slam into him. The ladder that was carefully perched against the white shingles suddenly has two people on top. The thing sways in slow motion and we start to fall backward.

Someone below yells, "Jump! Let go!" Deegan releases the ladder and disappears, which makes me scream more.

As the ladder comes crashing down, it collides with a big blue sheet and then the ground. The wind is knocked out of me and I can't breathe. Panic makes me close my eyes and then I feel a hand on my shoulder. I want to scream but I can't. A moment later, my breath returns and fills my lungs. And then I scream—loud and clear—and very late.

When I calm down enough to figure out what happened, I hear someone saying, "She seems a little unstable. I mean, first she was wearing a shower curtain in the hotel lobby and now this." Concern rings her voice, but it hits me like a gong over the head.

I'm still lying on my back as the fireman asks my name, then checks to make sure I didn't break any bones. My camera, on the other hand, is cracked and unusable. It went flying when I fell with Deegan. It's not insured because I haven't paid them this month. I lay there for a moment, staring at the stars wondering why I can't pull it together. I mean, I did this to Nick and he didn't crush the Shelter Island Fire Department.

Deegan is never going to talk to me again. Humiliated, I sit up and cringe. The crowd of people surrounding me drops their voices to whispers, but continue to stare at me. Well, everyone except my mother who has already gone. She probably hoped I would die on impact or spontaneously combust. She handed me a book when I was in fourth grade about spontaneous human combustion. Apparently, it happens at random and the only thing left is a pair of smoking feet. I took it as a hint.

A fireman is talking to me. His face is haggard, like he's done this too many times today. I shake his hand and tell him I'm fine. He tries to get more information from me, but I walk away, too embarrassed to stay there.

CHAPTER 22

By the time I get back to my room, they've got the doorknob fixed. Again. The evil redhead from reception is there along with a maintenance man.

She sneers at me. "It's unusual to have the same door act up twice in one day."

"Yeah, well, what can I tell you? I have bad luck. If you'll excuse me, I'd like to go to bed. I just fell out a window and don't really feel like talking." I go to push past her, but Red blocks me. I imagine her evil horns growing out of her scalp as she slaps her hands on her hips.

"There are cameras everywhere. If we find out that you tampered with this piece of hotel equipment—"

"The doorknob."

"Yes, then we will fine you and charge you for all related damages and expenses. Do you understand?" She says the last three words as if I hit my head, but I didn't.

I get into her face. "If you had footage, you would have used it by now, so don't go getting all up in my face without any proof. You should be worried that I could sue the hotel for crappy doors and shitty windows. Don't tempt me." I shove past her and slam the door in her stunned face. Her mouth forms that little O that people make when they're shocked. Since the tampering was done in a discrete way, they didn't see me. I guess they didn't catch Nick either. Rat bastard.

Look at that. He's gone up a level from plain bastard to rat bastard. I throw my busted camera on the floor and flop down on the bed, draping my arm over my eyes. My hair covers his pillows and linens. I didn't bother to pick out the twigs and dirt before I lay down. I wiggle on his white sheets making them a ghastly shade of brown in certain spots, before rolling off onto my pallet on the floor.

I can't stop thinking and I'm scared to death that I'm going to lose everything. The guy is using me and I'm attracted to him. Great combo. Wonderful. Deegan doesn't come by to see if I'm all right. No one does. I'm the crazy shower curtain girl who fell out a window. They avoid me like the plague. It's clear that I don't fit in here, but I never fit in anywhere.

It's well past two in the morning when Nick tumbles into our dark room. A giggling voice is there with him. I hear her purr, "Come on, Nick. Just for the night, no strings."

"Sorry, baby, but I can't. Roommate." He sounds remorseful. Good. I hope he chokes to death and dies.

"So, throw him out. I promise to make it worth your while." I hear silence, then giggling, and then more ragged breaths. I hate her. I hate him. I hate everyone. Grabbing my pillow, I pull it down over my head so I don't have to listen, but it doesn't help.

Nick moans and I despise the fact that I love that sound. Deep in my belly something twists and I wish I were the one making him react that way. I tug the pillow tighter and chase away the thought. He's not forgiven and never will be. He kept me from Deegan, broke my camera, and pretty much tossed me out a window.

After more kissing noises, Nick backs into the room and closes the door. Slut on heels click-clacks down the hall and, despite the carpet, I can hear her leave. Before looking at the bed, Nick sits down on the edge and grabs his hair in his hands.

He remains hunched over like that for too long. Something's wrong. I watch his back expand with every breath, but the man doesn't look up. He remains like that, rubbing his temples. When he speaks, his voice is barely audible.

It's not meant for me, he's saying it to himself. "I can't do this."

CHAPTER 23

The following morning, I'm up before Nick. It's not even sunrise. I slip out of the room and head for Sophie's room with an arm full of clean clothes. I knock lightly. Bleary eyed, she opens the door. Her annoyed expression changes instantly and she tries not to laugh. "Fall is my favorite season."

"I thought I could fly, what else can I say? It didn't work out." I make light of last night otherwise I'd cry. We both know it.

"You and that book." She's talking about Peter Pan. Sophie's the only other person who understood why I liked it.

The whole thing is about freedom and innocence, purity of passion and hope. She closes the door and follows me into the room. While sitting down on her big bed, she says, "I thought you'd leave—jump on a plane and fly away after high school. I never thought you'd stay in New York, not in a million years."

I shrug my shoulders like it doesn't matter. Plane tickets cost money and if I ever get the chance, I'm heading directly for London to see the statue of Peter Pan in Kensington Gardens. That day may never come. I answer her with a sarcastic tone, "Yeah, well, you know I want to hang out in Babylon and become my mother. It's easier to do with her nearby."

Sophie snorts and pats the spot beside her on the mattress. "I thought you skipped out on me last night."

I want to tell her that it was Nick, but I bite my tongue. I have no idea why. "Sorry, I fell asleep. Not flying really takes it out of you."

She laughs. "You mean falling."

"Yeah, that." I lay back and look at my best friend. We're both quiet for a moment, before I ask, "Do you love him? Would you jump out a window for him?"

She smiles fondly. "In an instant."

"Would you ride a rhinoceros? Pet a pachyderm? Slay a sloth?"

More laughter and she shoves my arm. "Very nice idioms."

"You mean alliteration, and yes, slay a sloth is my very own. It's trademarked, so don't go using it in your wedding vows." We both laugh and Sophie falls on her back next to me.

We stare at the ornate ceiling and the way each curved line is painted in gold with spiraling flowers in the center. Someone stood there and painted that. Artists are so important and so totally shafted. Sophie's room is the bridal suite. Everything is ornate and over the top pretty in here.

"I'm going to miss you." Sophie shoves my arm and I grin at her. "Well, I already missed seeing you naked. How was the shoot? Was Ferro a creeper?"

Sophie's sweet face pinches. "What are you talking about?"

"Nick, he said he was shooting your boudoir pictures last night. He came to get me and then, well, I fell out the window." My eyebrows creep up my face. "He didn't shoot you?"

Sophie shakes her head. "No, and I never said he could. What's going on with you and him, Sky? Sometimes you get this look in your eye, like you might chop off his head, and other times, well—"

"There are no other times."

"I'm your best friend, Sky. You can tell me."

I don't want to. I don't want to admit it to myself. Nick played me last night. It's the second time I was stunned by his warm lips and hot hands. The thing is, I know it's all an act, but my heart seems to have missed that memo. "He's attractive, that's all. Besides, you never answered my question."

"You never answered mine." Sophie sits up and looks at me, her hands on her knees. The bed dips where she sits as she waits for me to mirror her. I do and look her in the eye. It's what we did when we were younger. It's the truth stance. You can't lie when you sit that way, feet tucked under your butt, and eye to eye with your bestie. "Do you like him?"

"Yes," I grudgingly bite off the word. "Do you love Steven?"

She smiles slowly. "Yes. He's quiet compared to you, Sky. That's all. He isn't like anyone I've ever known. Isn't that what your husband is supposed to be?"

I nod. "You're right." I take her hands, "And I'm glad."

"About Nick?"

"There's nothing to tell. He used me."

Sophie drops my hands and blurts out, "Oh my God! You had sex with him!"

"No! He kissed me." My voice warbles and I look away.

"Oh no, Sky…" The way she says my name makes me look up. "You love him."

"I do not! He's just getting to me. It hurts because he doesn't think of me that way. That's all."

Her eyes sweep my neck. "Where's your kiss?" She means the thimble that's usually on a chain around my neck. I didn't put it back on after Nick gave it back to me. It seemed like a good time to stop dreaming that the right guy would come along. It happens for some people, just not me.

"I took it off." I don't explain and start to get up, but Sophie yanks my arm back.

"We are not done yet. You've worn that since you were twelve years old. Every day. Why'd you take it off?" Sophie stares me down, but I can't tell her. "Sky, say it. I won't judge."

"I gave it to him. He gave it back. He calls me Wendybird." Sophie's jaw drops. She gets it. I stand and stomp around the room, not understanding why he locked me inside last night. My eyes sting like I might cry.

I blurt out, "I thought he understood me and I know he's at least read that book. He knew the thimble was a kiss and he gave it back. And when he kissed me for real, I could barely breathe. My heart beat up when his beat down. I noticed. Everything was perfect, but he's a player and I'm not. It's one-sided, Soph. Don't read into it, please. You'll only make it harder for me."

"What do you mean?"

I cringe. "Your cousin's bet…"

"Yeah, what about it?"

"Nick and I have a second bet going." I stare blankly as I talk, my eyes slipping over the closet doors and their golden pulls. "I bet some things I shouldn't have." My heart beats faster thinking about it.

"What'd you bet?"

Turning, I look her in the eye and cringe. "Me."

Sophie's eyes turn into basketballs as she gasps. "Why would you? How could you do that? I mean, are you insane? You like him, so you bet against yourself so you can sleep with him? What the hell is wrong with you?" I've never seen her this mad.

"I don't know, Sophie. I just know that when Nick is around, I feel more alive. I feel this pull to him. It's like he's a magnet and I'm a piece of scrap metal. I can't stay away from him. His voice makes me warm and happy—at least, when he's not pretending to be his usual, asshole self."

"So, the guy who sang like a fool so you could get your shot—you love that guy?"

I nod. "Yeah, but he's buried under mountains of Ferro pride and power. That guy is a shadow. He's not real."

"Is this a Peter Pan metaphor?" Sophie blinks at me and her brow scrunches as she tries to figure it out.

"No, Soph. It's a real life problem. How do you fall in love with someone you barely know, a person who's hardly there anymore?"

Sophie's big eyes are filled with remorse. She shakes her head and her dark hair falls over her shoulder. "I don't know, Sky."

"He told me that he's here to crush me. He's not going to stop stealing my customers until he drives me out of business." I glance up at her. "But he didn't do your lingerie shoot?"

"No. On that note, I think we better make sure you win that bet and take some pictures before everyone wakes up." Sophie smiles and grabs her wedding night lingerie.

"Really?" I try not to smile.

"Yeah, anything you want. You have to win this bet. I assume you get something worthwhile if you win."

"He closes his shop and jumps off the bridge of his choice." I grin and glance out the window. The sun is rising.

Sophie laughs, "And you'll be there to take a picture."

"Exactly."

CHAPTER 24

The light is perfect and Sophie is cooperating more freely than I'd ever dreamed. We get the typical bedroom shots out of the way in no time. When she agrees to go outside, I know I'll nail this. I'm a little bit worried about using the older camera body and lens, but my better one is trash.

Sophie looks beautiful in her white wedding lingerie. She had a real corset imported from England with steel boning. In other words, think Golden Age of Hollywood, knock out, stunningly beautiful. I lit the room that way even though old-fashioned lighting is considered harsh now. One light in a dim room, highlighting Sophie in that cream-colored corset, lace-topped thigh-highs, satin heels, and a sheer robe that trails the floor. I have her hold onto the bedpost and walk around the room like I'm not there. When she's looking at the bed, I call her name, and her dark eyes go wide as she glances up at me. "Yeah?"

It's a photographer's trick. Saying someone's name makes their eyes widen and the direct light showcases her pretty irises. I'm going to make some of the images black and white. She looks like a movie star from the forties.

"Okay, that's about it, unless there's something else you wanted."

"Actually, I do. I want you to win. We are heading to the cove now. Just give me a second to change." Sophie tries to pull the metal tabs on the front of the corset, but it's too tight.

"Hold on." I unlace her and she disappears into the bathroom. When she comes back out she's wearing a silky cream-colored piece of lingerie. The front dips down low, like to her belly button, and there's no back – just pieces of string. The satin on the bodice flares into a skirt with a slit that goes way up to the top of her thigh where I can see a single garter. She's removed the rest of her stuff—no stockings, no heels, and from what it looks like, no bottoms. She offers an awkward smile. "I know you wanted moonlight, but the sun isn't very high yet. Will this work?"

"Yes!" I'm so excited that I literally squeal. It's contagious because Sophie responds with giggles. She grabs her coat and I take a few towels before we leave the room. It's still early and hardly anyone is moving around yet. The halls are empty, but we don't want to risk running into anyone in the elevator. We sneak to the stairwell, trying to reach the shore unnoticed.

That's when I hear his voice, Nick's. He's on the landing below. The carpeting muffles the sound, so he doesn't know we're there.

"I know and I am." He speaks firmly, but I have the clear distinction that someone is talking down to him. Silence and then, "Nothing will change and it's already done, just make sure she doesn't find out." He sighs and I peer over the railing. He's wearing the clothes he had on last night. They're rumpled like he slept in them. Nick runs one hand over his head and growls into his phone, "I said I can do this and I have. This is the final nail. I told you I could do it, so you better hold up your end of the deal." I back away from the railing when he ends the call.

Nick is sitting on a step and staring at the wall. It seems like this is the last place he wants to be, and right now, this is the last place Sophie wants to be, but it's too late. Nick stretches, sighs and looks straight up—our eyes lock.

He was talking about me. He had to be. Even so, I can't shake this feeling that something's off. Nick is all business and always has been. I decide that I'm going to act like nothing's happening. I take Sophie's hand and drag her reluctantly past him. I expect him to pelt me with questions, but he doesn't.

When I brush past him, Nick is still sitting on the step. He reaches for my hand, stopping me. "Sophie, can you give us a minute?"

"No, she can't." I pull away and all the magical qualities of his touch fade. It's the worst feeling in the world.

Nick doesn't move. "I'm sorry about last night and I'm glad you weren't hurt. I never thought you'd go out the window."

I turn and look first at him and then back at Sophie. "There are some people who are worth jumping for."

He offers a weak smile. "I suppose there are." He stands, dusts off his pants, and adds, "And I'm done with pranks. Again, I'm sorry."

No! What is he doing? He can't act sweet one second and stoic the next. I'm starting to gnash my teeth, but Sophie grabs my arm. "Come on, Sky."

I nod and follow her out, ranting non-stop about Nick. I must have said his name forty times by the time we reach the cove. "Sophie." I whine her name like I'm twelve again. "What do I do with him?"

She smiles in a very un-Sophie-like manner, all sultry, and says, "Kick his ass and then take it from there." Sophie's dark hair hangs down her back and looks black against her pale skin. "So, should I dive in or what?"

Grinning, I reply, "I have a few ideas. How much skin do you want to show?"

"Whatever you think works. Let's go. I'm freezing."

"All the better for sexy pictures, my dear."

We shoot in the early morning light. I expect Nick to come, but he doesn't. I promised I wouldn't shoot without him. I'm wondering if that makes the bet messed up. If he doesn't shoot boudoir pictures of Sophie, then, while judging, she'd know these were all mine. I say what I'm thinking and she puts her hands on her hips and gives me the duh face. "So, we're cheating?"

"No, just bending things in your favor—just a little bit." I raise a brow at her. "Okay, a lot. You're going to win. Period. I'm picking one of these."

"You realize you have to display the winning picture in the lobby, right?"

Sophie's brows come together. "What? When did you say that?"

"I didn't. Your ass faced cousin did." Sophie's smile falls. "Well, then these might be a little revealing for that."

"I'd do it just to piss off my mom."

Sophie laughs, "You totally would, but I don't think I could. Mr. Stevens—uh, Dad—will never look at me the same way again." My face burns and I look away before she notices.

"So, do you want to do this last part or not?"

"I don't do halfsies." Sophie slips off the rock and into the water. Her gown sticks to her porcelain skin and becomes completely transparent.

I tell her what to do and she does it. Sophie hugs the rock, climbs on the rock, lays on the rock, and then floats by me with a serene smile on her face. The red lips, black hair, blue water, and golden sunlight make it completely perfect. And that piece of lingerie, being totally sheer, makes the shot sexy as hell. I wish I had a picture of me like this. Sophie looks like a goddess—I'll have to ask Amy which one. That's the picture, though, the best one I'll take, and no one will see it because of what water does to white. But that's what makes it sensual. If she hadn't been clothed, it wouldn't have the same effect. The image is sublime and totally perfect.

I pull my friend out of the cold water and wrap her in towels. She hands me her wet nightgown and asks me to have the hotel have it cleaned and back in her room by tonight. "Done."

As we walk up to the path together, Sophie says, "Don't sleep with him. It's one thing if you lose the bet—which was the stupidest bet ever—but it's another to give him your heart, you know? Don't do it, Sky." She's worried about me. I can see it in her eyes and I don't want today to be about me at all. I've been selfish as it is. She's getting married tonight and I've been blathering about me all morning.

"I won't." I give her a hug and hurry her inside, but the lie burns my tongue. I didn't mean to fib, but it's one of those things that you realize is false only after you say it. Nick already has my heart. He took it when he gave me that kiss.

CHAPTER 25

I'm running late. The bride's brunch is going to start in less than an hour and I'm not dressed yet. Nick is still in the shower. Banging on the door, I yell, "Hurry up! I need to get in there, too!"

"I slept on mud because of you. Wait your turn." His voice is sharp, so I back away and pad over to the dresser. He's left a watch that cost more than my car, his wallet, and the change from his pocket, all spread over the smooth surface. I can't help it. I pick up the coins one by one and flip them over, looking for a double-sided coin.

Nick comes out, shrouded in steam, with only a towel around his waist. His dark hair is tousled and his chest is perfect. It leads up into a perfect pair of shoulders and down into a firm waist. Each ab is defined like he does sit-ups all day long. How can he look like that? Nick notices my wandering gaze. "Soon, Sky. Just wait." He winks at me with that Ferro grin and I want to kick him.

I toss his change at his chest. "Jackass."

"Flirt."

"Bastard."

"Siren." That one makes me flinch. God, the words he chooses are too much. They're exactly what I want to hear.

I step closer to him and smell his aftershave. The scent could make me orgasmic. What is that? Pheromones of Ferro? "Rat bastard."

He smiles softly and looks down at me. "You said that already."

"No I didn't. It's an entirely different level of bastard. You're king of the bastards."

He maintains eye contact and leans so close to my mouth that our lips brush, "It's good to be king."

I shove his chest. "Of all the stupid things to say."

He grabs my waist and pulls me close. "I'm a guy, Sky. I have balls, not breasts. What'd you think I was going to say? That you're my shadow and I had no idea how lost I was without it? Do you think I'll ask you to sew it on so we can fly away together? Is that what you want to hear?" Holy shit. It feels like he sucker punched me in the stomach. I tear myself away, refusing to show how much his words affect me. Nick watches me with those cold blue eyes. His gaze narrows as he reaches for his shirt. "I'm not that guy, stop looking at me like I am."

Screw it. I'm saying whatever I want. "You don't know who you are, so I can look at you however I damn well please. Right now, this look means I'm disgusted."

"Disgusted? Really?"

"Truly. You act like you're this giant asshole, but I don't understand why. To what means? Why do you think you have to be somebody else?"

"I don't. This is me." He jabs his thumb into his chest.

I'm wasting time fighting with him, but I don't want to stop. Shaking my head, I lower my lashes to the floor. "No, it's not, but you're right about one thing. You have no shadow, no anchor holding you down so that when the darkness comes you're totally fucked."

"There's no such thing as a soul."

"Yes, there is. There's good and evil, right and wrong. You're still young enough to decide what kind of man you want to be. You don't have to become your father. No one is holding a gun to your head."

Nick's shoulders stiffen and he stops breathing. Bull's-eye. I hit the man's sore spot and he's refusing to acknowledge it. "You have no idea what kind of man I am or what kind of hell I had to go through to get here."

"I'm sure, poor little rich boy who doesn't have to pay rent."

"It's not like that." He grabs my arm and pulls me toward him. "Don't assume you know me, because you don't. If I rip your business to shreds it's because you were too weak to fight back, so don't blame me when the whole thing falls apart."

My mouth is hanging open when he stops talking. I storm into the bathroom, slam the door and crank on the water. When I stand in front of the mirror, I grab the porcelain sink firmly with both hands and look at myself. I'm not weak. Is he serious? Is that why he was able to crush me so easily? I don't want to be that kind of person, the type who cuts off her competition's head based on speculation. He still thinks I'm a snob because I tossed him out the first day we met. I can see it on his face. Why is he holding onto that? Is that why he's doing this to me?

My eyes glance down to the sink. As I reach for my toothbrush, I see a silver coin. I lift it and look at one side. Tails. Then I flip it over and slap it down on my palm. Heart racing, I peer under my hand. I don't want to look. Please tell me that he's not that kind of man. My gut is screaming that he isn't, but his actions don't mesh. At the same time, everything he does is inconsistent. Nick Ferro is a walking, talking enigma. He seems kind, but cheating with something like this is wrong. This means he doesn't care about me at all, that he's been playing me the entire time—kiss by kiss—until I'm so distracted he can blindside me. If this is a double-sided coin, I cringe, not wanting to bear the thought. It means I can't trust myself, that I was totally wrong about him and his character. I already know he's playing hardball, but there's a difference between playing for keeps and cheating. Please, let it be a normal coin. Slowly, I lift my hand away and stare at the shiny object.

Tails.

My jaw quivers and my heart falls into my shoes. It's just like Deegan said. Part of me wants to go out there and throw the coin at his face, but I remain in the steamy little room devising a better idea.

After today, Nick Ferro is going to wish he never met me.

CHAPTER 26

When I get out of the shower, I expect Nick to be gone, but he's still there sitting on the bed like a saint. I hate him, but I hide it well enough. I have to crack the door to let the steam out or my hair won't dry right. I'll look like I licked an electrical outlet. As it is, the humidity has it misbehaving. I'm surprised no one's mentioned the massive frizz bomb I inherited from my father. Since his hair is always cut short, no one notices. My hair usually hangs long down my back, but on days like this—when it feels like a cloud is sitting on the ground—my hair transforms into Medusa locks.

Amy. I smile to myself. She's running the studio for me while I'm out here. I'd originally planned on staying the entire week. After the wedding tonight, Sophie and Steven will take off for the airport. They encouraged the guests to stay a few extra days and hired entertainment and wonderful meals, but I'm darting home as soon as Sophie's foot lands on the limo floor.

That will take place after she chooses the winning picture. Nick and I will have an hour to process our favorite shots and then someone will mix them into a slideshow. That's when I'll see which picture my best friend and her husband choose, and who is better at shooting weddings—me or Nick the rat bastard.

When I crack the bathroom door, Nick says, "Sophie said she wanted to talk to us and not to leave until she comes by."

I stick my head out the door. It's still wrapped in a towel. "Yeah, right."

"Do you really think I would have waited for you? You've been in there forever." Nick looks at his watch. Brat.

"I'm leaving when I'm dressed."

Nick shakes his head. "Guess again." He tosses me my cell phone, which was next to my blankets on the floor. There's a text message flashing.

It's from Sophie: I NEED TO TALK TO YOU AND NICK; STAY IN YOUR ROOM UNTIL I GET THERE.

I glance up at Nick, wondering if he can send a fake text.

"What?" he asks, like he's done nothing wrong.

My plan to screw him over is already in action. When Sophie comes by, I'll get something from her but I wish she'd let him leave the room. That wasn't part of the plan. I'd talked to her earlier and asked her for a few things that I know she has in her emergency bride kit. Sophie over-prepares; she packs everything and anything. This time, all that extra crap will come in handy. I mean, what kind of bride needs superglue? I smirk, thinking about drizzling it all over Nick's lens, so it can't focus. He won't realize it until it's too late and the man didn't bring any back up equipment. If he's cheating, I have to ditch the rules, too. I can't lose this bet with Sophie's hideous cousin or Nick.

"Nothing," I say like he doesn't have any effect on me at all. "When did she say she'd come by?"

He shrugs. "She didn't."

I nod and head back into the bathroom and blow out my hair, put on make-up, and then dig through my suitcase and pluck a pair of panties that are too pretty to wear when no one else is going to see them. I should wear them, because they'll make me feel confident and sexy. The front is black lace with some hot pink peeking through. The sides are double straps that connect at a bow in back and attach to a G-string. Like I said, not the kind of thing I'd normally wear to work, but I grab them anyway. I take the matching bra that gives me insta-boobs and amazing cleavage, before pulling on a non-descript black blouse and pants.

The photographer shouldn't be seen— at least that's my method. I wear leather-soled shoes so I don't make a sound when I shoot a wedding. Everyone should be looking at the bride and not paying any attention to me. It's amazing how some photographers don't respect that tradition. They're up in front, blocking everyone's view, and being as outlandish as an elegant elephant in a tiny pantry. That's not me.

Just as I pull my hair back and pin it up, there's a knock at the door. I come out of the bathroom just as Nick stands. He pads toward the door and pulls it open. Sophie and the crazy redhead are standing outside. Sophie is half dressed. Her hair is done and her makeup has been applied. She had someone from the city come out to do it. I rush toward her and give her a hug. Nick steps back into the room, giving us space.

Sophie laughs and hugs me back. "I'm so excited, Sky! I can't wait."

"I'm so happy for you. I really am."

She breaks from the hug and steps forward into the room. There's a different expression on her face, one I've never seen on Sophie before today. I don't know what to make of it. Nick's gaze flicks to the side to see if I'm getting a read on my best friend, before returning his focus to Sophie.

"I thought you'd want some getting ready shots," Nick offers. "What's going on?"

Sophie puts her hands behind her back and rocks on her heels. The Red Devil remains behind her staring at me like she wants to rip my head off and turn it into a salad bowl. "Well, I wanted to make sure that you both had what you needed."

What is she doing? "Yeah, Soph. We're fine." Better than fine. "Did you bring what I asked for?"

"Actually, I wanted to talk to you about that. If you don't mind, I need a moment alone with Sky. Can you guys hang out in the hallway for a second? I promise it'll only be a second. Thank you so much for leaving the desk to help me." She says the last part to Red.

Red smiles like a saint. "Of course. It's your wedding day. I'll be right outside." The woman wanders down the hall. Nick walks past me, as if he doesn't like this, but does as Sophie asks and leaves us alone.

That's when I get the truth. Sophie's expression shifts from happy to displeased in a snap. She places her hands on her hips, which pulls at her silk robe, opening the front so I can see the top of her corset. "Skylar Thompson, I will not let you do this." She gets into my face and scolds me, throwing me way off. Sophie doesn't have a mean bone in her body. She's never raised her voice to me, ever, but now she lets me have it.

"I have to."

"No, you don't. Just because he's a cheating piece of slime, doesn't mean you have to become the same. You worked your ass off, honestly, to get to where you are. If you cheat and do this to him, you'll regret it. And I'll lose every ounce of respect I have for you. This isn't you, Sky. Don't sabotage him, break his gear, or glue his seat. I know you have something planned for this, and I'm giving it to you because I'm not your mother, but if you go through with this," she sucks in a huge breath and spits out the words, "I'm not sure I want to be your friend anymore."

Sophie's words hit me like knives and suddenly I can't breathe. There are no words. I just stand there with my mouth hanging open. Sophie grabs my arm, opens my hand, and shoves the tube of super glue into my palm. I glance down at my hand and then back up at her. "Sophie, I—"

She shakes her head and lifts her hand to silence me. "There are actions that change people, Sky. There's no going backwards after this. Make your decision carefully or you might not like who you become." Her dark lashes drop to the floor as she turns to the door. Sophie twists the knob and beckons Red and Nick back into the room. "Please take their gear to the chapel. Put Nick's on one side and Sky's on the other."

Nick offers that Ferro charm, "Sophie, I hardly think that's necessary."

His charm slips off of Sophie like a drop of water. "No, I really think it is." She glances at him for a moment and then looks back at me. "You two are cut from the same cloth. You're just too stubborn to see it. If you did…" Her voice trails off and she laughs, practically blushing. Her innuendo makes me step away from Nick. I can't believe she did that. "Well, it'd be a sight to see."

Red requests our gear. If I'm going to superglue his camera, I'll have to get to the chapel first. Sophie watches me for a moment before turning on her heel and closing the door behind her. Nick and I stare at each other.

After a moment, he asks, "What was that about?"

CHAPTER 27

"I don't know," I lie, folding my arms over my chest and staring at them. I can't look him in the eye, not after I do this to him. I wonder how he can look at me as if he's done nothing wrong. I'm not that person. Sophie knows I'm not, but I have to win. I have to. What am I willing to do to ensure it, especially when Nick is cheating? My gaze flicks up to his. "Sophie doesn't like us squabbling, I guess."

He hesitates and offers, "She seems like a good friend."

"She is, she's the best. Sophie's the kind of person I strive to be, but I fall short. She's like Snow White, Mother Teresa, and Tinker Bell all in one body." The thought makes me smile. "I honestly didn't know she had that in her. I've never heard her say anything like that before, like ever."

Nick's brow furrows and his arms fold. He stares blankly at the place where Sophie stood, then looks back at me. "Do you think it's bridal jitters? It doesn't seem like it to me. She's one of the nicest people I've ever met, to tell you the truth. Steven is a lucky guy."

I look up at him. "Yeah, he is." Our eyes lock and we look at each other way too long. Suddenly, I'm very aware of my heart and it kills me that Nick isn't who I want him to be.

My phone chirps and breaks the moment. I glance down. It's a text from Deegan.

SORRY I DIDN'T CHECK ON YOU LAST NIGHT. MY ANKLE NEEDED A LITTLE ATTENTION AFTER ALL THAT. HOW WOULD YOU FEEL ABOUT MEETING ME BEHIND THE CHAPEL TONIGHT?

I smile at the phone. Nick notices and walks over. Before I can hide the message, he sees it. "You know he's using you, right? You seem a little bit too nice for him." I turn and stare at Nick. I don't know what to say, so I just continue looking at him. The action makes him squirm. He looks away from me, and glances back every few seconds, searching for the words to explain. "There are guys that prey on girls like you, that's all I'm saying. Be careful, okay?"

I don't blink. I gape at him as my arms fall to my sides. My eyebrows lift up into my bangs and disappear. "Are you bipolar or something? Why bother acting like you give a rat's ass about me, when you don't? Deegan's not like that. He's a better man than you'll ever be." A little harsh, yeah, but I'm not taking pointers from Nick Ferro. Screw that. My body tenses and somehow I'm in his face.

Those blue eyes remain locked on mine. He doesn't flinch or deny anything. "I know you hate me. I didn't expect you to listen. I just hoped you would." He turns away and sucks in air like it's his dying breath. "Come on. We better get down there."

I follow Nick to the door, absolutely livid. It takes every ounce of restraint not to fight with him, but the wedding is in an hour and he's right. We need to get over there. There are shots that Sophie will want and I don't want to miss them.

Nick grabs the handle and twists. I see him pull the door and his shoulder jerk. "What the…?" Nick repeats the action, but the door won't open.

At first I think he's messing around, trying to make me smile or something, but he's not. "What's the matter?"

"It's stuck."

"I see that." Shoving him out of the way, I try. The door doesn't give. I glance at Nick and we both dart for the only other way out—the window.

The building has older windows, the kind with the metal lock that swivels between the top and bottom panes, holding them together when it's locked. He tries to unlock it, but the metal doesn't move either. Nick glances at me with fury in his eyes. "Did you do this?" He practically yells in my face.

Tilting my head to the side I give him a look that says his question is stupid. "Yes, I locked the window and the door so we'd be stuck in the room together. Are you mental?" I snap. "Of course I didn't do it! Move, let me try."

"You're too weak. It's been glued shut."

After pushing and pulling on the lock I turn slowly and look at him. "Glued?"

"Yeah, look at the metal. There's super glue all over it. You can see the white haze it leaves when it dries." Nick points and then walks across the room to grab something while I stare blankly from the window and to the door.

She didn't. Oh God. If Sophie thinks I might do something I'll regret for the rest of my life, would she do this? I would have said there was no way, but I must have given her the idea. She locked us in here. I have to get out. I have to win. If I don't show up at her wedding, I'll be the worst best friend ever. Screw the bet. I can't do this to her. I mutter, "I didn't think she..." Panic laces my voice. Nick studies me speculatively. His eyes take in every detail from my rounded shoulders to the way my fingertips barely touch my lips.

"What? Tell me."

I don't know why, but I answer him. "I think Sophie did this."

"No, she wouldn't have. That's insane." Nick shakes his head. "It doesn't matter anyway. We're getting to that chapel. If we pull the lock off the frame, the window will open. We can call down for help or I can lower you down. Whatever you want." I watch his face for a second, wondering why he'd help me. It's like he can read my thoughts, because he says, "No matter what you think of me, I'm not a total asshole. I'm not ruining your friend's wedding by neither of us showing up."

Nick tries a pencil under the lock, but it crumbles under pressure—as do the next few objects he tries. He needs a piece of metal. That will pull it apart. "What if Sophie doesn't want us there?"

"Then she would have fired us. She's just trying to get us to slow down and stop fighting. If we get there at the last second, we can't fight. She's smart. I'll give her that. What bride walks around with super glue?" Nick shakes his head and breaks another pencil. Shards of wood go flying.

I hand him a letter opener I found in the desk. "Try this."

He takes it. "Thanks. This should work." And it does. Although it bends into an L-shape, Nick is able to pry the metal lock completely free from the old wooden window. It was held in with little nails that go flying as it comes free. Nick grins at me and says, "Come on." I step closer to him as he pulls on the sash.

It doesn't move.

He pulls again and swears, banging his fist into the wall. "She glued it." He curses again as his fingers trace the entire lower windowpane. The glue goes all the way around.

"No. She wouldn't." My voice is too high, too airy. I sound desperate and hurt. I guess I am. Nick steps back to let me see for myself. I trace the glue with my fingertips, panic building in my stomach.

Nick pulls his phone out and calls someone, but says nothing. A moment later he hangs up. "The front desk isn't answering."

"Sophie hi-jacked the desk clerk. She took her to the chapel. Is there a number for the chapel?"

Nick shakes his head and sighs. "No, there isn't. Unless we want to break the glass, we're trapped."

I glance at the window. "It's not going to break."

"How do you know?"

"Because Sophie threw a wooden music box at me when we were little. I ducked and it hit the window. The window didn't break."

"So we use something heavy."

"It was heavy. That thing was a brick, that's why I didn't just catch it. We both thought the window would break, but it didn't."

Nick looks desperate. His brow is covered in beads of sweat and he's pacing the floor like a mad man. He runs his hand over his forehead and through his hair. With every turn he repeats the action. Something has him on edge, like this wedding is a life or death event for him. He mutters to himself, trying to think of other ways to get out of the room.

I grab my phone and text Sophie: I WON'T DO IT. I'M SORRY. PLEASE, LET US OUT.

I know in my heart she did this, but my friend doesn't respond. I press my eyes together in frustration and throw my phone at the wall. The casing protects it so it just falls to the floor with a thump. Nick turns and sees me, tears forming in my eyes. "I'm going to miss my best friend's wedding."

I sit down hard on the edge of the bed. In this moment, I hate myself. I was willing to become someone I swore I'd never be, but Sophie saw it. I didn't. She sacrificed her wedding pictures because her best friend was too dumb to listen. I ruined her memories. She won't have any. I plant my face in my hands and try not to cry.

I wouldn't have been that selfless. Can she even still be my friend after this?

Nick's frantic pacing stops when he sees me. At first he says nothing, then, shucking his tux jacket, he comes and sits next to me on the bed. "This is my fault. I know you probably won't believe me, but for what it's worth—I'm sorry."

I laugh, but it's bitter. "That's amazing. How do you make it sound so sincere?" I sit up straight and wipe the tears from my eyes. "I have to know. How do you lie to someone's face and pretend that they matter to you when they don't? It's a business skill that I'm obviously lacking and desperately need."

Nick turns away quickly so I can't see his face, but I don't stop. "Tell me, Nick. After you hose this business, I have nothing, like, literally nothing. My best friend isn't going to talk to me ever again, and I'll lose my business because I couldn't outmaneuver you. You stole my clients and drove my business into the ground. Now, I have to sit here with you until someone comes and lets us out. Somehow, I'm guessing that will be

Sophie with a chainsaw tomorrow morning!" By the time I'm done, I'm crying, yelling, and laughing. The image of Sophie in her wedding dress with a chainsaw is funny. I can't help it.

My emotions explode and splatter everywhere. I can't hide them anymore. That's when I shove Nick's shoulder. "And you. Why'd you have to cheat? I could have handled everything up until that point, but you frickin' cheated!"

He turns to look at me. "Just what did I cheat at? If I did cheat I'm unaware of it. I play angles, crush hopes, and mislead— but I don't flat out cheat."

"Well, isn't that refreshing?" I stare at the floor.

Nick grimaces and then inhales deeply, before running his fingers through his hair. "I can't change who I am. I'm a Ferro through and through. You knew it when you first met me—that's why you tossed me out without a packet. You saw through me every moment after that. You knew I'd take you down, but you put up a helluva fight."

"Not that it matters—I've already lost. Without pictures from this wedding, I can't keep my shop open." I feel numb. A goofy, sad smile consumes my face and I look up, and blurt out. "That isn't even the worst part. The worst part is Sophie doesn't trust me anymore. That's why we're locked in here. She didn't want me at her wedding." I sniffle and then laugh awkwardly, glancing at Nick who's intently watching me. "I've never had a friendship end this way before."

"It's my fault, not yours."

"No, it's not. I was going to do something to you and I told her." I straighten and run my fingers through my hair until I reach the place where it's pinned up at the back of my head. Smiling sadly, I tell him, "I was going to get back at you for the double-sided coin."

He looks confused. "What are you talking about?"

"The coin toss, smart ass. You used a double-sided coin."

"I did not—I don't operate that way. If I were to try something, it would be untraceable. A fake coin is amateur hour.

I'd get caught." Nick is watching me intently. The tight fake smile fades from my face as I think back to the other night.

I stand abruptly, walk to the bathroom, and come back with the few coins I found by the sink. "These are yours, right?"

"No, I thought they were yours."

I lift the double-sided quarter and show it to him. "This isn't yours?"

He laughs, like I'm kidding. "Of course not, and if it was, I wouldn't be stupid enough to leave it out. Sky, I used a regular coin. You called it, not me."

I think back, staring at his beautiful face as I remember that night. I can't help it. I smile a little. "You didn't cheat?"

He shakes his head. "Someone doesn't like me very much, huh? Story of my life. People hear Ferro and run the other way. I suppose this time it was my own goddamn fault, but it hasn't always been this way."

I'm leaning forward with my elbows on my knees. Nick is sitting close to me, but not touching, leaning back on his arms. "What do you mean?"

He slips and lies on his back, tucking his hands behind his head. "I'm the middle child, like, the classic middle child with middle child syndrome and all that shit. My parents pretty much considered my brothers and me clones of each other. After graduating high school, we were each given options of acceptable professions, but my chosen careers didn't fit. I chose my own path, instead. The thing is, I know the family is ruthless. My aunt enjoys being like that, flaunting her power like a freaking monarch on crack."

His voice sounds different, like he's lost. This isn't the certain Nick Ferro who's been promenading around me for months. It's the man I glimpsed inside that other guy. I hear his voice and I can't help but turn and look at him. Nick speaks to the ceiling, almost as if he's afraid to look at me.

Nick clears his throat and continues, "I thought she was crazy, but my Dad's the same way. They're clones, my aunt and my dad. They think the same way and have the same expectations. So when little Nick Ferro discovered he had artistic abilities, they were squashed. No Ferro is permitted to have such a mundane job. But I couldn't stop learning—that would have been like trying not to breathe. I just can't. So I learned photography and I learned some other things."

"Some?" I prompt. I know damn well that he knows a lot of artistic things. I can see it in the few pictures he took.

He laughs once, softly, "I'm trying not to exaggerate. Somewhere between high school and graduating with my masters, that artsy guy disappeared. Now I'm all gusto, charisma and charm. I have to be. It's on 24/7 and I have no idea why I'm telling you all this." He sighs and looks over at me. "Ah, right, it's because you already know. You have this gaze that's unnerving, you know. It's like you can see through me and tell I have no soul." He shivers and, although I know he's making light of it, I can see he believes what he says.

I turn toward him and pull one foot up onto the bed. Looking down at him, I say, "You have a soul—it's not a thoughtless compliment, it's the truth. If you didn't, you couldn't take photographs the way you do."

Nick watches me a moment too long, then lowers his gaze. Those dark lashes obscure his blue gaze. He opens his mouth with a fake smile and then shuts it again. "I can't bullshit you. In all this time, you're the only person I can't fool. It's like you're bullshit-proof."

The comment makes me laugh. "A wonderful quality to possess, indeed."

"It is, but there's more. Tenacity and genuine concern and care for the people around you—even when life doesn't treat you fairly, even when I didn't treat you fairly."

I mash my lips together and ask him again, "Why me? And don't say because I'm the best. That's bullshit."

Nick's smile fades. "I had to prove myself. You were the job."

"What?" I straighten and look at him because that sounded totally wrong.

Nick shakes his head, "I love your dirty mind, gutter girl, but that's not what I meant. I was given a target based on my current set of skills. The goal was to destroy your business in ninety days and complete every contract I received. I had to make sure you closed your doors and never opened again."

He mashes his lips together and hands me his phone. "You were chosen for a reason, by my father, so I could work at the family company. My objective was to prove to him that I am ruthless enough to handle business matters, no matter what. He pinpointed someone I admired and told me to destroy her."

Taking his phone, I look at the picture he has pulled up. It's an article about me printed in Babylon's newspaper, a paper so small I thought no one ever saw it. My picture is there along with a shot from one of my bridal sessions. They did a story on me because "the portrait was sublime for a photographer so young." They felt my level was unusual for my age. I continue to stare at the article, unable to wrap my head around what he's telling me. "But this was almost four years ago."

"I know." He reaches for his phone, but I accidentally flip it to the next picture and stare. Shock fills me from head to toe and I drop the phone on the floor.

Nick sits up quickly, worry flashing through his eyes. "I'm not a stalker, Sky. I just saw your work when I was getting my degree and fell in love with it. I guess when I met the legend and got shunned it hurt a little, so it lessened the sting when you were assigned as my target." He lowers his eyes like he can't stand what he's done.

A Ferro was infatuated with my work? I lift his phone from the floor. "May I?"

Nick swallows hard and nods before getting off the bed and heading toward the window. He slips his hands into his pockets and looks outside at the blue sky and setting sun. Sophie is probably walking down the aisle right now. I push the thought away and take a deep breath. I flip to the next picture, it's another piece of my work. I flip from image to image, finding a spattering of work from other artists—most of whom are long dead.

My throat is tight, but I manage to say it, "I didn't give you a folder because I liked you too much. I didn't know who you were, but I knew I couldn't be in the same room with you and not..." I stop suddenly, unable to finish. I can't imagine what it must have felt like to him that day. People fall in love with the art, and hope the artist isn't a jackass. I seemed cruel to him, dismissive. The corner of my mouth pulls up into a half smile as Nick turns around.

His eyes widen and lock on mine. I can't breathe. Someone stole all the air from the room and I'm going to die. "Finish your story."

"You finish yours." My voice shakes as I speak, but the tremor is spreading.

Nick holds my gaze and steps toward me. With each step, he tells me a little bit more. "I idolized you. I watched your Facebook page and Twitter accounts. You appeared funny and smart, kind and talented. When you tossed me out without a second look," he works his jaw and finally says, "I took it as a challenge. I copied everything you did because it obviously annoyed you and, well, because it was brilliant. Every client I stole gave me satisfaction, because I thought you were the fake. I was all too happy to rip your business to shreds, idol or not. My father applauded me. He didn't think I had it in me, but I did—and he knows this wedding is your final straw."

Nick is standing in front of me, a step away like there's an invisible barrier between us. He takes a deep breath and asks, "Why'd you throw me out? You couldn't be in the same room with me and not...what?" Fear drips down my spine like ice. I stare at him, wide-eyed, wanting to run, but Sophie glued us in this room. I look everywhere but at Nick, until he kneels in front of me and touches my cheek lightly, repositioning my gaze until I look him in the eyes. "Tell me. Please."

My jaw hangs open, flapping and gasping. I want to crawl both away from him and toward him at the same time. I'm an emotional mess, overstressed, and this is too much. He's been trying to destroy my business all this time because he thought I hated him. My God. My voice is a whisper, "I knew I couldn't be in the same room with you without touching you. I was attracted to you. A lot. So, I threw you out. I couldn't shoot the wedding of the only guy I've ever met whose mere presence made my pulse race like that. It was a bad idea. In the first three seconds you were in my shop I was enamored with you, and the more you spoke, the more I liked you. I had to throw you out. I had to."

"You liked me?" Nick's voice is soft, surprised. He blinks those dark lashes and watches me like this can't be happening.

But it is. I nod once and the gentle caress of his hand on the side of my face nearly undoes me. I've liked him so much, for so long, that this kills me. "If you don't destroy me, what happens?"

"I have no job and get cut off from the family."

"So, being stuck here with me now means that you're..." Oh my God. I can't say it.

So Nick does. "I'm ruined. Disowned. Pick one. My family doesn't accept me the way I am, but you did—even though I wore ratty clothes and was covered in dirt. Skylar." When he says my name, my skin prickles and my head feels light. He's so close he could kiss me, but he doesn't. Instead, Nick kneels at my feet like I'm some sort of goddess and touches my cheek.

"We have to get you down there." I start to move, but his other hand comes up.

Nick cups my face. "I'm not leaving this room."

CHAPTER 28

"But, you can't. You already beat me, Nick—just call the front desk and go downstairs. I haven't got enough gas money to get home, I didn't pay my insurance and my best camera broke. There's no way I won the bet, and the bet was the only thing that could save me." Nick doesn't speak. His eyes rove over my face again and again learning every inch as I speak. I plead with him, but he doesn't listen. He stays there at my feet, holding my face and making my heart pound harder and faster. "Go! You have to. My business is already over. There's no point in both of us losing everything we wanted."

His hands slip off my face and I think he's going to leave, but he doesn't. Instead Nick turns and says, "I never wanted this. I only did it because of the way you treated me."

"I'm not the kind of girl that would crush on a guy if he belongs to someone else. Nick, I was young and handled it wrong. I'm so sorry, but sorry doesn't change what's going on now."

"It does." He rubs his face and shakes his head. "I'm not that guy. I found my shadow, my anchor, and she's sitting right here beside me. She gave me her kiss and I gave it back. I hurt her over and over again, and still she's here, listening, even though I don't have a chance with her. Not after all this."

Sophie's words make sense now. She saw it and I didn't—we were both turning into the same person—someone jaded and heartless. Neither of us chose it, it just happened, and Sophie stopped it. I don't know what to do. I feel like it's my move, but I'm frozen. Whatever I say next changes everything. I could destroy him. When he speaks, there's a tremble in his voice.

My eyes search the room and land on the thimble next to me on the nightstand. I take it in my hand and fiddle with it. Nick turns and looks at me. I stand and walk over to him, but this time instead of a snide comment, I hold out the object.

"I've worn this every day since I was twelve, until I gave it to you." It's an innocent statement. I reach for his arm and lift his hand, placing the symbolic kiss in the center of his palm and closing his fingers around it. Nick watches me intently as I lift his other hand and bring it to my lips. My body is tense and I can't breathe, but I also can't stop. Pressing my lips to the center of his palm, I close my eyes for a moment while I savor kissing his hand, and then pull away.

Tension lines Nick's body, like he can't believe I just did that. It was innocent and sexy at the same time, and if the man keeps looking at me like I'm a goddess I'm going to cry. Watching him, I shrug my shoulders like it doesn't matter when

Nick doesn't respond. He stands very still, staring at me.

Worry that it was too weird or wrong fills my chest. Just when I'm about to turn away, he takes the thimble and presses it to his lips. "You see through me. I'm a sheet of glass to you." I'm breathing too hard. We're standing nose-to-nose when he slips the necklace into his pocket. "Don't break me, Sky."

"Ferros are unbreakable," I say. "As soon as that door opens, everything will change." I feel his eyes moving up and down my body and I want more. I want him, but I'm afraid. I can't tell what's real and what isn't because this feels like a dream.

"It will. You'll go back to being my idol and I'll keep my distance the way I did before."

My stomach twists as tingles spread over my skin from head-to-toe. The way he looks at me says everything. "What if I don't want that?"

"Then show me," he whispers. "Show me want you want, Skylar."

CHAPTER 29

I'm nervous and have trouble finding the words. "I'm not a one-night-stand kind of girl."

"Neither am I." He reaches for me and tangles his hands in my hair on either side of my head, watching me, waiting.

"Deegan was a fluke."

"You don't have to explain."

"I've only ever been with one guy before, and I—" I'm breathing so hard that my chest is rising and falling. Every time I inhale, my chest brushes against his and I die a little. It shoots feelings through my body that I haven't felt in a long time, but they're magnified. It's different, better.

He strokes my hair, pulling out the pins and letting it fall loose down my back. "And you what?"

If this doesn't make him run, nothing will. I drop the bomb and wait for him to jerk back. "I was in love."

I can't read him. Nick stays perfectly still, looking into my eyes. "And now?"

"That's not fair."

"Life's not fair. Tell me. Say it, Sky."

I'm about to swoon. I finally know what that word means. I feel desire consuming me and if I don't kiss him soon, I'm going to die. He's a breath away from me. I could just lean in and close the gap. I don't have to say it. "You say it."

He blinks at me, as if deciding something, and then everything changes. The tension between us heightens and he leans in, whispering in my ear, "Am I so transparent to you?"

A shiver runs down my spine. When he presses his lips to my neck, I gasp aloud. Nick moans in response and my knees go out. He catches me in his strong arms and sits me on the side of the bed, assuming nothing. When he looks up at me, the pull is so strong that the space between us closes without thought. Suddenly his lips are on mine, soft and perfect. Nick brushes his mouth against mine again and again, slowly, waiting for me to let him in.

His hand lifts to my cheek and he angles my head back. I feel woozy, like I'll fall back and I want to pull him down with me. I fight it, remaining upright until the kiss deepens. My tongue flicks against his lips and he's there, ready to taste me. I shiver and Nick wraps his arms around me, holding me tight, kissing me fiercely. I gasp and tear at his shirt, trying to get it off. Nick stops and yanks it over his head. When he glances at me, I reach up, slowly pulling my blouse over my head and revealing the lacy black and pink bra beneath. I'm so glad I didn't wear granny panties today.

Nick's gaze lingers on my body, dipping down first to my waist and then back up to my eyes. "Are you sure?" I nod, unable to speak. Nick smiles slightly and lowers those sexy dark lashes. The look he has on his face is so beautiful, so shy, and so unlike him. "I need to tell you something, but you have to promise to keep it a secret."

"What?" He has my attention and the butterflies stirring in my stomach calm down for a second.

Nick glides his hand over my cheek and traces a finger down my neck, following the curve of my body, softly, lightly. As he trails his hand over my breast and down to my waist, he leans in close and makes sure I can see his eyes. He stutters, trying to find the right words, and it's so cute that I can't stand it. I kiss his cheek and pull at his belt. "Just tell me. Say it, Nicholas."

He shivers. "Oh God."

"Tell me."

Those blue eyes are dark with desire. Nick's lashes lower, then lift, and when our gazes lock, he confesses, "I love you. I can't believe I'm holding you. This is a dream, Sky."

"I love you, too." I laugh as a tear rolls from my eye. "I wanted to hate you, but I just couldn't."

"I'm glad." Nick presses his lips to my neck and the world blurs away until it's only him and me.

Nick spreads kisses across my neck and down my body. Inch by inch, he moves his mouth lower and lower. I feel dizzy with lust. I have no idea where my pants went or when they came off. Nick's hands rove over my skin and cup my butt pulling me toward him. As he does so, he finds my mouth and kisses me hard. My eyes are closed, lost in lust, as I kiss him back. The butterflies in my stomach swirl into a tornado, fluttering upward into my head. I don't think, for once I feel and only feel. I allow myself to let go and be lost in the moment. I drop my defenses and say whatever comes to my lips, as Nick pulls us toward ecstasy.

He's gentle with me and takes his time, letting me get to where I need to be before he tries anything like what Deegan tried the other night. It feels so different—good different. My body responds to his touch and when I feel my bra disappear, I'm not afraid. I don't think about anything but him and me, and his touch on my skin. Nick's mouth teases me until I can't take it anymore. I cry out and feel warmth pulsing between my legs.

Nick watches me as I find my release and when I open my eyes, he's smiling. "You can do that without me even touching you?"

For a second my face turns red, and I bury it in his shoulder, hiding my shame. He pulls back and smiles down at me. "No, no. That's not what I meant. Don't be ashamed of that at all. It's beautiful, sensual, and I can't tell you how much I want to be with you. I want to make you writhe. I want to hear you call my name and dig your nails into my back."

Nick hooks his thumb around my panties and pulls them off. Before I can ask about protection, he has a condom out and on. Our slick bodies glide together, twisting, and tangling, while climbing higher and higher as his hips rock against mine. I'm lost, floating away, letting him do anything he wants, but what he wants is me. He treats me like he'll never get another chance to be with me. Every inch of my body is kissed. Every place is touched, every curve is learned, until I can't stand it anymore.

I cry out his name over and over again, rocking in sync with him until we both shatter.

CHAPTER 30

Nick's been lying on his side, totally naked, brushing my hair away from my face. "Are you all right?"

I nod. "I'm perfect." I kiss his cheek and he grins at me. I'm feeling light, floating away like a little cloud.

"I'm going to get a drink. Do you want something?" There's a mini-bar in the room, and neither of us has touched it until now.

"Water, please." I lie on my back and smile at him as he pushes off the bed.

He leans in and kisses the tip of my nose. "You made me fly, Sky." Smiling, he watches me for a moment and then walks across the room.

On the way, he begins to pick up our scattered clothing. When he lifts my pants, something falls out—the bottle of super glue. Nick picks it up and before I can notice what he has, he looks back at me, suspiciously. "You did this?" He holds up the bottle.

It isn't until I sit up that I see what he has. For a second I'm afraid, very afraid. "No, I was going to do something, but Sophie chewed me out and I never had the chance." Damn. That came out wrong. After we realized we were locked in a room together, I decided against sabotaging his equipment. We both fell down a slippery slope, but this looks so bad.

Nick takes the glue and quietly places it on the desk. When he looks at me, his eyes are narrowed, and he doesn't speak. Instead of going to the mini-bar, he pulls on his jeans, boots, and an old T-shirt. Then Nick walks over to the door and kicks it so hard that the jamb splinters.

"Nick, wait!" I jump up, taking the sheet with me. "Wait!"

But he doesn't stop. He turns the corner and runs down the staircase without a word.

I'm still standing in the door, wearing nothing but my sheet and feeling like scum, when my phone rings. I walk toward it. AMY is flashing on the screen, so I answer. She never calls. "Hello, what's wrong?"

"Sky, I'm glad I caught you. We have problems. I tried to handle everything else, I mean I did handle everything else, but there's been a shitstorm of crap since you left."

"What do you mean?" I sit down hard on the edge of the bed as she fills me in.

"The fire marshal showed up a month early and fined the hell out of us. I knew you were strapped, so I paid it. Don't say anything. I know you're too proud to accept help, and besides, you helped me when I fell flat on my face. But since then it's been non-stop. I've handled everything, Sky, but this—I can't do it. I mean, I tried, but you're going to see it as soon as you come back." Amy sounds like she's ready to crack.

"What happened?"

"The sewer line to the shopping center backed up and ruptured in your store. It must have happened during lunch. I only left for an hour, but when I came back I found two inches of sewer water all over the floor. It was gushing everywhere. I called the city and they said it was the landlord's issue, so I called the landlord and he shut it off, but Sky—everything is ruined. I called the insurance company. I swear to God, I tried to handle it, but they said your policy lapsed. I don't know what to do. I can't afford a clean-up service and no one can be in here right now."

I blink rapidly as she speaks and try not to cry. Nick did this, I'm sure of it. While he was covering me in kisses a pipe broke and destroyed my store. I manage to ask, "What about Nick's store? And the rest of the shopping center?"

"The break in the line was by your store. They weren't affected."

My chest feels hollow. He ripped out my heart and stomped away. I don't cry when I say it. "Flip the sign to closed and leave. I'm sorry, Amy, but I'm not going to be able to recover from this. You'll have to find a job somewhere else."

Amy gushes apologies and tells me that I might be able to come up with something when I see it, but I know she's just trying to keep me in one piece until I get home. "It's okay, Amy. I knew this was coming. Thank you for everything. I'll see you when I get back." I end the call and cry into the pillow. It still has the scent of the man who told me he loved me, while he stabbed me in the back.

CHAPTER 31

I shower and dress, packing up the things that I brought into the trunk of my huge car. The sun has set and the reception is in full swing. My dad is still wearing his suit. It's a little too snug and pinches under his neck and arms. But he looks nice all dressed up. "Skylar, are you leaving so soon?" His face is pinched. He knows I wasn't at the wedding, but he doesn't ask why or what's wrong. There's this thing he does, it's like he can tell when I need him and he just quietly shows up. He usually knows what to say without adding to my anguish, so I don't hurry away from him.

"Yeah, Dad, I have to," I say, not making eye contact with him as I speak. "A pipe broke at the store and it's a huge mess. Amy said she needs help and she never asks for help. I need to go back."

He tucks his hands under his armpits and stands in that dad pose he sports when I'm ready to burst into tears. "My tool kit is in my trunk. Let me go get it for you. Maybe there'll be something you can use."

I don't have the heart to tell him no, so I nod and say, "That'd be great."

Daddy walks off while I dart inside and up the staircase to grab the last of my things. I'm so afraid I'll see Nick, and I can't deal with him now. I need to go. *Stay focused. Stay calm. Cry later.* I chant my mantra over and over again, planning on singing angry 90's music all the way home. The people on the ferry will totally ignore me. It'll be awesome. The Jagged Little Pill album is already queued to play on my phone.

When I get to my car, I dump the rest of my stuff in the trunk and slam it. That's when I see dad toting a red toolbox toward me. When he's by the car, he says, "Sometimes things don't work out and the reason has nothing to do with you, or how good you are."

Damn it. My eyes sting, but I blink back the tears. "Thanks, Dad." I take the toolbox and kiss him on the cheek.

"Sure. I'll come by the shop when I get home. We'll fix it, Sky." I nod and smile at him. There's no point in telling him right now. Besides, I have a feeling he knows I've fallen on my face and lost everything.

Now the only decision left is whether or not to retrieve my crappy camera with Sophie's boudoir pictures. It's sitting in the chapel and I don't want to risk seeing Nick. I can't just leave it there, so I decide to sneak around in the dark by staying off the main path. I move through the parking lot like a crook, and around to the side of the hotel. Keeping off the path, I take the long way to the chapel, ensuring I won't see anyone.

Staring at the ground, I kick a rock and wonder how things could have gotten so messed up. My heart is gone and my chest feels empty. My anger has melted away and I don't know where it went. It'll probably spring up at an inappropriate moment and make me look even crazier than I already do.

There are massive boulders on both sides of me, and I know I shouldn't walk this path after sunset, but I really don't want to talk to anyone else before I leave. I weave my way in and out of trees and boulders, following close to the shore, while making sure I'm still hidden in the shadows. For a moment, I think someone is behind me, but when I look back, nobody is there.

I continue on to the chapel and just before the turn I should take to come up behind it, I hear a twig crack. I whirl around, heart racing, and expect to see an ax murderer, rusty blade in hand, but instead it's just Deegan. "Hey, Sky. I thought you were never going to show up."

Confused, I stare at him and then finally remember his text message. "Oh, yeah. Listen, today didn't go as planned."

"Tell me about it." He falls into step beside me and slips his hands into his pockets. "But that's no reason to waste a perfectly good night, right?"

Sex with Deegan? Now? Can he not read me at all? My shoulders are slumped forward and my eyes are all puffy. Any idiot could tell that I'd cried long and hard. "Not tonight, but thanks."

"Hey," he grabs my arm and pulls me with him toward a rock. A tree grows right along side of it, so you can't see anything else. "Oh shit, don't tell me that asshole nailed you instead of me. Is that where you've been all day? I thought the cheating thing would have sealed the deal. Guess you take whatever you can get." Deegan waggles his eyebrows at me.

"What are you talking about?" My brain still feels foggy, like I'm missing something.

"I put that coin in your room when housekeeping was there. I said I forgot something in your bathroom and I left the coin on the sink for you to find. I thought you were the innocent type, and was sure a cheater would turn you off. Guess not." He tries to kiss me, but I won't let him.

Pushing my hands against his chest, I try to shove him away.

"Deegan, cut it out." My stomach sinks. This feels wrong, even though I know him. He wouldn't hurt me. He's just messing around. I push him again, but he doesn't back off.

"Don't be like that, Sky. Let me help you forget whatever's bothering you." In that second he changes. Deegan doesn't listen to me, pressing harder against me as he gropes and grabs my ass. At the same time, his lips come down on my neck. It's what we did last night, but it feels different now—it's unwanted.

"You're bothering me," I try to shove him away, but he doesn't move. "Deegan, stop! It's not funny anymore!" My voice is a little louder this time, but it's nowhere near a scream. I shift to knee him in the groin, but the guy pins me against the rock and clasps his hand over my mouth.

"Come on, Sky. If you were going to give it away the other night, why is this night any different? Relax, okay?" He's watching me, trying to see if he can move his hand.

~ 234~

Every hair on the back of my neck is prickled. Deegan's other hand is lingering by the hem of my skirt, lifting it higher and higher. I nod, and his hand slips away. "Let me do this my way and I'll make sure you like it. If you don't, you won't like it at all. Understand?"

He's too close. I try to act like I'm going to answer him, but the air that fills my lungs for the scream inflates my chest. He feels it and I barely shriek before he's crushed me back against the rock again. All the air rushes from my lungs and I can't yell. The little yelp is swallowed up by the dark night, and my heart races harder. Sweat drips down my neck and I feel paralyzed.

"Fine, if that's how you like it." Deegan turns me around, but manages to keep my mouth covered. He's right up against me, lifting my skirt and pushing my face into the stone. I try to yell, but I can't move, and he has me pinned so tightly that I can't breathe. When I hear the zipper, I snap. Without thinking, I bite into his hand and don't stop until I taste blood.

He screams, "You bitch!" before he lets go. My skirt falls and I try to run, but he catches my wrist. "You fucking little whore!"

"Let me go!" Now that he's finally uncovered my mouth, I have no breath. I can't belt out a death scream, I can barely talk because his grip on my throat is so tight. I kick at him and drop to the ground. That's what they said to do if someone's trying to take you, right?

Deegan drags me for a second and stops. "Fine, you want it this way. I'll give it to you, Sky." I try to crab crawl away from him on my hands and feet, scurrying backward. I'm incoherently crying, saying things that don't register in my mind. He lunges at me and gets hold of my ankle and drags me back toward him. When he straddles my hips and pulls up my skirt, I start bellowing so loudly that he slaps me across the face. Blood spatters from my wound and I'm temporarily silenced. He grins, right before he positions himself to push in. "You know what they say, right? It's usually someone you know."

I can't move. I close my eyes and expect him to rape me and take what he wants, but there's a rush of air, a strangled sound, and then nothing. When I open my eyes, he's gone. I sit up and frantically look around. Deegan is rolling with someone, another guy. Deegan throws a punch, but the other man is beating the crap out of him. I stand shaking, unable to move or speak. Punch after punch is thrown until Deegan stops fighting back.

"Stay down, you mother fucking son of a bitch!" Nick's voice rings out. I try to see his face, but it's obscured by a red ball cap. He looks up at me and I just stand there shaking. A second later I start to cry. Nick doesn't come to me. He doesn't comfort me or hold me. Instead, he keeps his foot on Deegan's chest and calls the cops.

CHAPTER 32

By the time the police arrive, Sophie and Steven are gone. Thank God. I don't even know if she's my friend anymore. The cops wrapped a blanket around me and told me to get counseling when I get home. I could just nod. I want to leave. Nick stays the entire time, but he keeps his distance. He tells them that he was walking on the street, on his way back from the chapel, when he heard me scream. When he got here, he did what he could.

The cop smiles. "You broke his ribs." Nick looks livid, so the officer explains, "I would have done the same. Fucking asshole." Then he gestures at me. "Make sure she's okay. She shouldn't be alone right now and it sounds like she's driving back home. She won't even tell me her name or her next of kin. Do you know her?"

Nick looks over at me and shakes his head. The cop rolls his eyes. "And I suppose you're Mr. Smith?"

"Yeah."

"Folks, we can't press charges if we don't have names. Are you pressing charges or do you want me to let him go?"

Nick answers for me. "She'll press charges. I'll call her attorney and take care of it. She's going to crack if you push her right now."

The cop shakes his head, "I need to hear it from her."

"What he said," I manage, pulling the blanket tighter around my shoulders.

"Okay, tell your lawyer to get on it or the guy walks." The cop takes Deegan away and suddenly it's quiet.

I stare at the ground, still shivering even though I'm not cold. I haven't said anything and I don't know how long I've sat, but when I look up, Nick is still there standing across from me.

After a moment, he says, "Sophie told me about the glue, and that you didn't do it. The tube in your pocket was full." I just stare blankly at him. "Sky, I don't know what to do."

My defenses spring back up. Every wall I've ever made juts up from within me and I steel myself. "I don't care." I drop the blanket and start to walk back to my car. With each step, I walk faster and take longer strides.

"Where are you going? Sky, stop." Nick chases after me. Running alongside me, he says, "I'm sorry. I thought you played me. I thought you were sincere and then I found out you weren't. What would you think?"

Livid, I stop, but a placid calm smile comes across my face. "Exactly the same thing."

"I can't fix this, can I?" Nick asks. I shake my head and look away after folding my arms over my chest. He's going to pretend that he had nothing to do with decimating my studio. Fine. The hell with him. "I deserve that, but you can't drive home by yourself."

"Watch me." I turn and walk away. Nick is careful not to grab me or touch me. It feels like I'm rattling and all the nuts and bolts that hold me together are coming undone and falling to the ground with every step I take. When I reach my car, I get in and slam the door. The window is down and I can't put it up until I start the engine. When I do, the car is so damn old that it takes forever for the window to go up. It slowly slides closed with Nick standing there. He could easily stop it, but he doesn't.

Instead, he says, "Wait, Sky, let me get someone you care about. Hold on." He looks up at the hotel, but seems torn.

I growl at him, "If you tell anyone what happened tonight, if you ruin Sophie's wedding any more than we already have…"

"Skylar, this wasn't your fault."

"Don't call me that!" The window finally shuts.

I throw the car into reverse and back out, but the parking lot is new and made for normal sized cars and mine is a monster. I have to pivot in and out and in and out nearly three times, and by the fourth time, I've wedged my car in between two SUVs with Nick watching. That breaks me and my forehead slams forward onto the steering wheel and I sob big, yucky, snotty cries.

Nick steps toward me and opens the door. "Move over. I'll drive you home."

I do as he says and lean into the passenger seat, as far away from him as possible. When we first leave, he makes a phone call to have all his stuff moved to the room. "Yeah, I'll pay extra. Just make sure you get the camera bags. Something came up and I had to run. They're on the path by the chapel." After that Nick is silent.

I lean against the door and fall asleep. The next thing I know, Nick is calling my name. "Sky? Sky, wake up." I glance over at him. "I don't know where you live."

"In the studio."

His jaw drops. "You're not allowed to do that."

"No one knows. It doesn't matter now anyway."

Nick pretends he doesn't know. "What do you mean?"

"Just go to the store." Nick doesn't say anything else. He drives down Montauk Highway until we come to the shopping center where his little studio is on one side and mine is on the other. The stench in the air is horrible.

Nick pulls up in front of the building and turns off the engine. "Sky, you shouldn't be alone right now."

"Go fuck a monkey, Ferro. I don't have time for you or your fake sincerity." I don't sound like myself, but I'm too upset to care.

Nick follows me to the store. "Hey, what are you talking about? Sky?"

I shove the key into the lock and pull the door open. The smell worsens, hitting me in the face like a wall. When I step over the threshold, I'm standing in rank water. It fills my shoes and shuts Nick up. I slosh to the light switch and turn it on. I might be able to salvage the table and chairs, but all the books and albums are toast. The biggest problem is going to be the back of the store. My shooting room had tons of stuff on the floor, including my bed.

When I glance through the doorway, into the back, I grab the wall. Everything is ruined. The room is filled with water and it looks like it came down from above and flooded the place. I stand there staring, and feel Nick looking over my shoulder. "Congratulations, Mr. Ferro. You decimated your idol. You can stop pretending you care now and go get a pat on the back from your dad. Oh, and all that bullshit you said to get into my pants was brilliant. You had me convinced."

I turn to leave, but he stops me by stepping in front of me. "I didn't do this. How could you blame me for this?"

"My store is the only one that got flooded. The city said the problem with the pipes was within the building, Nick. I may be younger than you, but I'm not that dumb. You got what you wanted. I lost. You win."

"Skylar, I didn't do this." He sounds sincere, but I'm too fried.

"Don't lie to me anymore! I can't take it!" I shove his chest, hard.

"I'm not lying."

"Just go." I turn away and look at the destruction.

"No, I didn't do this." Nick picks up his phone and calls someone. "The tenant in unit 281 was flooded out earlier today. Yeah, this is his son, I have the unit across from her. What happened?" He's quiet for a moment, and the longer the silence stretches the narrower his eyes become. His jaw tightens until it looks like it's going to crack. "Thank you." He hangs up and looks at me. Nick sloshes through the sewage, yanks one of my signs off the glass and marches outside.

The only reason I follow is because I can't breathe inside. Nick walks to his studio, opens the door and flips on the lights. I watch him grab a razor blade and scrape the name of his studio off the door. When he's done, he takes a piece of tape and hangs up my sign. When he comes out, he tosses me the keys. "It's yours."

I catch them, but I don't believe him. "Very funny."

"It's not a joke." He's storming away, like he's going to take my car. Nick grabs the driver's side door and holds out his hand. "I need the keys. I have to go have some words with my father."

"You're making this up, Nick."

"Think whatever you want, Sky, but I need to go take care of this. Right now. And you can't sleep in your place. You'll die, the smell is so bad."

"You did this to me. It happened while we were together. There's no way you can convince me that you didn't know or that you couldn't stop it." I ball my hands into fists at my sides.

"I know I've lost you and I almost lost myself. You brought me back and made me realize I was drifting. You don't believe me, I know, but I need to go make this right. Please let me." He holds out his hand, waiting for the keys to my car.

"I'm going with you."

CHAPTER 33

We drive forever, backtracking out east. Again. Nick puts gas in the beast. I'm barefoot because my shoes absorbed the nasty water. They were stinking up the car so we tossed them in a dumpster. Nick had this waterproof stuff on his boots so all the sewage rolled right off. Someone needs to make that for people. When life gets shitty, you can spray a little on your emotions and they all go back to the way they were before.

I'm not that naïve, but I can wish. We arrive at the Ferro family mansion in the middle of the night. Nick parks my ugly car right in front and rushes up the steps.

Then he's inside and bolting up the stairs. I'm ready to drop, but I manage to follow him through the twisting halls.

He heads straight into a room with tall ceilings and leather walls. Bookcases are scattered about, along with a few sculptures that cost a small fortune. Nick's father, Darren, is behind his desk, still dressed, tie loosened and talking on the phone. "Jared, things aren't that simple and you know it." When Nick rushes in, his dad stops talking abruptly and says into the phone, "I'll call you back."

"What did you do?" Nick asks. His shoulders are tense and he looks madder than he did before.

His dad looks at Nick and then his gaze drifts back to me, dipping to my bare feet. "Secured your position and taught you a lesson at the same time. You had only a few days left and, as of this morning, Miss Thompson's business was still open. You don't want to lose your place at the company, do you? Acquisitions are hard and you did very well up until now. Being around the acquired business's owner is a mistake. You proved yourself to me. We just had to finalize everything to make it look all right with the company. I can't have people accusing me of nepotism." He laughs and adds, "Or that the Ferros are going soft."

"Her business is not closed. It's been moved to my storefront. I lost." Nick slams his hands down on his father's desk so hard that it makes me jump.

A knowing smile crosses Mr. Ferro's face and he addresses me, instead of his son. "He's had a crush on you for a long time. Do you have any idea how much determination and stamina it takes to destroy the business you admire the most? I watched my son tear you apart, brick by brick. Why you're standing in my office in the middle of the night, shoeless, is beyond me."

I walk across the room and stand next to Nick. "I'm standing here because your son loves me. I'm standing here because he gave me his store. My business's name is on his front door."

Mr. Ferro smirks. "You think you can get him so easily?"

Nick cuts in before I can answer. "She doesn't want me." The words ring loud and clear. Nick leans in by his father's face. "And I don't want you."

He laughs. "Nicholas, you're being ridiculous. You're going to walk away from everything and for what? A girl that doesn't share your affection?"

Nick is already at the door. He turns back and shakes his head. "No. I found my soul over the past few days, and I'm not going to work with you and have it sucked out again."

I follow Nick through the door and hear his father say, "If you leave this house, never come back."

Nick walks faster toward the front door. That wasn't fake. I look over my shoulder and then rush at him just as he's about to step outside. "Wait!" I pull Nick's arm and stop him. "You can't walk out."

"Yes, I can. It's a step and I'm gone."

"But, you're a Ferro."

"And I wish that I wasn't. If I stay here, I know who I'll become and it's the man sitting behind that desk. I meant what I said up there. I lost myself, but over the past few days, you brought me back. I'm not staying here and changing who I am to please them again." He laughs. "The Ferro fortune is cursed—the papers say that—and they're right, because you have to give up your soul to get it. I'm done here and I'm not looking back." Nick walks outside and takes a deep breath of night air, like he's been a slave and now he's a free man.

CHAPTER 34

The ride back to the store is awkwardly silent. He just threw his life away, or found it. I wonder if he has any money or if he plans on becoming a hobo. On the way, I tell him to divert to my parent's house since they're still at the hotel. I can't take his store. I have no intention of doing so.

When we go inside, the smell of my childhood home hits me hard—lemons and Lysol. My mom is a clean freak. Even if I put everything back exactly where it was and make it sparkling, she'll know we were here.

Nick looks around. "You grew up here?"

"Yeah, I'm Baby Oops. My mother kind of resents me ruining her body after she finally got it back again."

Nick looks at the pictures on the walls. There are several of my siblings and only one of me. I'm wearing a cap and gown with a plastic smile. It's my high school graduation picture. He notices there aren't any others. I know he does, but he doesn't comment on it.

We go up to my old room. It looks exactly the way it did when I left because my mother said I would fail and would need a place to go when it happened. I don't tell Nick, but he's moving like he's walking on egg shells. He finally asks, "Do you want me to call Amy? Or someone to stay with you? I can't leave you alone, Sky. Too much has happened to you today."

I flop down on my old bed. "Then don't. There are blankets in the closet. I call dibs on the bed."

He makes a spot on the floor with blankets and a pillow, silently, before he turns off the light. I hear him tug his shirt off and slip under the blanket. When I roll over, I look down at him. His hands are tucked under his head and his eyes are closed. I watch him for a minute and then try to sleep, but I can't. I keep trembling and silent sobs randomly choke me.

After a few hours, I'm sure Nick's asleep. I slip out of my bed and lay down next to him. His eyes open and we watch each other. I finally ask, "You really love me?"

For a moment he doesn't answer. Finally he says, "I'll always love you."

"What are we going to do?"

"We?" he asks, and those gemstone colored eyes look so soft, so vulnerable. He touches his pocket like he's checking to make sure he has his wallet, but that's not what he's checking for.

Smiling softly, I nod. Tears form in my eyes and roll down my cheeks. "You still have my kiss in your pocket, don't you?" He offers the most beautiful smile I've ever seen and those dark lashes dip before meeting my gaze again. "So, yes, we. Plus, I'm your shadow. We belong together.

You can't separate a guy from his shadow, he'll float away."

Nick's eyes flick between mine intensely, before he asks, "Do you still love me? After all that? Sky, don't do this because you pity me. I couldn't bear that. It's less painful to know I've broken things beyond repair, that I had you and lost you, than having you stick around because you feel sorry for me." His finger swirls around the thimble in his pocket. I'm not sure he knows he's doing it.

"It's not pity." I manage, certain it isn't. After everything that happened today, I know it's nothing like that. When Nick came out of nowhere, I wanted it to be him. When he drove me home, I wished I could lean into his side and he could wrap his arm around me, but I was too afraid, too hurt. Now he's here and I've heard the whole truth and I love him more than I did before. "And I'm not taking your store."

He grins and fiddles with the blanket. "Yes, you are. I owe you a store. Besides, they look the same. No one will notice." He glances up at me, and I laugh.

For once, I feel like I've found my home and it has nothing to do with the bed or the walls. It's the man who's with me. Shyly, I ask the question again, searching for the truth, needing to hear it from his lips. "Do you love me?"

"I love you. I love you, Skylar. I love you today, I loved you yesterday and I'll love you tomorrow." He says it again and again.

I finally inch toward him and let him wrap his arms around me. "Nick?" He kisses my brow and snuggles into me.

"Yes, my love?" he kisses the top of my head and strokes the hair away from my eyes, before looking down at me.

"I love you, too."

CHAPTER 35

The next morning we both shower and head back to the studio. I flinch when I see his car out front. "How'd that get here?"

"I had someone bring it."

I glance at him. "How? I mean, I don't want to pour lemon juice on your circumstances, but didn't that cost a lot? How'd you pay for it?"

He laughs. "I'm not poor, Sky. I've been saving my own money for a long time, cash I earned myself. I've been working since I was fourteen. I invested some of it and as you said, I was over here rent free. The old man made me sign a lease and actually wrote $0 on the line. However, he did not say I couldn't sublet the space, so I am—to you. There are two years left, and it's all yours."

My jaw drops. "Are you still Ferro-filthy-rich?"

He laughs. "No, no private jets for us, but we can get an apartment, buy clothes, and eat. What's that called? Middle class?"

I nod and smile, watching him as he walks around and pulls our gear out of his trunk. "Come on, let's process what we have from Sophie's wedding."

"Nick, I can't take your store." But he doesn't listen. He walks inside, sets things down and starts turning on lights before turning to see me standing in the parking lot, gaping like a fish.

He holds out his hand, "Well, then let's make it our store. Work with me, shoot with me, live with me, love me..." Nick's hand dangles in the air as he reaches out to me.

My stomach twists because this will change everything, but it's a good, warm, feeling and I'm not scared anymore. Reaching for his hand, I say, "Yes," and allow him to hold onto me tight. Nick kisses the top of my head, and then my temple, and finally my lips. He lingers there, kissing me softly and making the butterflies in my tummy swirl with glee.

"Come on."

We work together for the next few days, sleeping in our studio until we find a little apartment down the street. It's closer to the water and it's on the second floor, so it's nice at night, when the moon is full. You can see the lake and watch starlight ripple on the surface. Nick finds me at the window sill, leaning out.

He slips his arms around my waist and kisses my cheek. "There's a text message from someone I know you'll want to see."

"Oh?" I turn around and take the phone. The smile fades from my face. I can't really tell what kind of message it is based on the first few words. Actually, it looks like she's texting me from her honeymoon to tell me off. I hesitate, not wanting to know if I've lost her.

Nick pulls me to the bed, our bed, and says, "Open it. You wanted to know; now you'll know."

Shoving my fear aside, I flick the screen and read her message. It starts with how disappointed she was when I asked for the glue. That was the part I could see on the screen before I opened it, and then the message apologizes for taking such drastic measures, but I mattered to her, and she couldn't let me become that kind of person. She was aware of the costs and the possible outcomes. When she heard my store was flooded, she sent the text. The last line of the message says: I'M SO SORRY. I HOPED THINGS WOULD WORK OUT AND YOU GUYS WOULD REALIZE HOW YOU FELT. IS NICK WITH YOU?

I type back three letters: YES

Nick is affectionate and touches me the way I've always craved. He takes the phone from my hand and pushes me back on the bed. "Please tell me you're done working. I have plans for us."

I laugh and push him off. "I have a few more shots to edit. I want them done by the time Sophie gets back."

He nods. "Can I see the one you're working on? Every time I walk by you shut off the screen."

Watching him for a moment, I consider his request. We pooled the wedding photos and have been editing them together, but I haven't let Nick see the boudoir shoot even though Sophie is clothed in all of them. I shot those based on how I felt about Nick, and it lets him see a little bit further into my mind than I'd like right now. "Maybe, but I don't think you'll like it. It's too dark, with an odd amount of juxtaposition."

He takes my hand. "Show me." Eagerness fills his gaze and I know he's excited about it for the same reason I'm frightened. Art is weird like that, it's a direct line to the soul. When someone doesn't like my work, it's hard not to take it personally. I'm not sure he'll like this. It's very different than the things I've done in the past.

I walk to the kitchen and pull up a chair in front of the computer, warning him of these facts.

Nick grabs a drink while the file opens and then walks over to me. The screen is off, and the finished picture is there waiting. All I have to do is press a button. My heart thumps, slamming into my ribs. "Ready?"

"Show me," Nick urges, and I hit the button. The image comes onto the screen and I close my eyes. I can't watch his reaction. The picture is Sophie, floating on her back, eyes closed, in the cove. Her satin gown clings to her pale body, revealing every inch the water doesn't conceal. The cream colored hem of her skirt billows around her ankles and off to one side of the picture. Dark hair swirls around her face and she floats with her arms by her sides, a single raised finger is the only way you can tell she's alive. It's life and death, beginnings and endings, darkness and light all caught up into one piece. It screams of utter confusion and sublime emotion. It felt like I'd drowned that day, but symbolized in that raised finger there was a flicker of hope.

Nick gasps and leans in closer. "My God, Sky. This is…" His jaw hangs open and I inwardly cringe. He hates it. I reach for the screen to turn it off, but he grabs my wrist. "This is the most amazing piece you've ever created. She looks like that old painting of Ophelia, but it's different, hopeful, like she'll float away and begin again. And the dress and the way the water surrounds her, she looks perfect, like a Greek Goddess."

Oops, I didn't think about that part too much before I opened the image. Sophie is dressed, but her breasts are clearly visible. It's like there's a layer of tissue paper to conceal her modesty and that's it. "I shouldn't have shown you this." I try to pull away, to shut off the screen, but he won't let me.

Instead, Nick pulls me to my feet and brushes my hair behind my ear. "Don't tell me that you're too shy to show me pieces like this."

"That's not it. This is my best friend. She looks perfect because she is perfect. Everything about her is perfect."

Nick tips my face up so our gazes lock. "Who made you so insecure? I want to kick his ass. I also need to tell you something. You need to see it, hold on." Nick clicks a few buttons and pulls up a picture of Sophie the way she usually looks and puts the two images side by side. "The woman you photographed may be your best friend, but she doesn't look like that. The woman in that picture, the heart and soul of that piece, is you. You made her body curvy with the water lines and shadows. The highlights from the sun illuminated her skin perfectly. This piece reveals more about you than her. I don't see a half dressed body in the water. I see you, your thoughts and fears, beautifully displayed in a context that means something to you."

"What do you mean?"

"That's your mermaid cove, right?"

"Yeah." Nerves shoot through me. I knew Nick was perceptive and the thought was in my mind when I shot the picture, but I'd not verbalized it to anyone, not even myself. I start to shake.

"This is symbolic for you, too. It's the end of childhood and the beginning of something else, something unknown. The mermaids only favored Peter in that book. They tried to kill Wendy and any other girl that went near their cove. The location of this portrait matters, because it reflects the end of one life and hopefulness of another. This Ophelia is not dead, she just needs to be revived—you needed to be brought back to life and leave some childhood notions behind—not all of them."

I stare at him feeling completely exposed, even though I'm dressed. I smile crookedly, awkwardly, "You see through me."

"Scary, isn't it?" Nick smiles and pulls me toward him. "I know how that feels. It haunts me every time I look at you. At the same time, it's freeing. I don't have to pretend around you. I already know who you are and I like what I see, childhood dreams, crazy mother and all—Sky, it just makes me want you more."

I throw my arms around his neck and he sweeps me up, taking me to the bed and showing me just how much he loves me.

CHAPTER 36

A few weeks pass. Sophie picks up her pictures and loves them. Her cousin defaulted on her bet since Sophie had no wedding pictures, so there was no money to be won. Amy is back working the front desk in the new studio and I've replaced all the albums that were ruined, and now my work and Nick's line the front room. We shoot together, but business has been slow.

Nick's father must have meddled with the news stories about my shops demise, because it sounded like I'd closed my store. Neither man has spoken to the other since their face off, despite his mother's constant urging. If we don't get a really good client really soon—someone who will refer us to more socialites—we are going to have problems. Nick and I both see it coming.

As I'm touching up an ad piece that I plan to hang in the front window, the front door chimes. I hear Amy's voice give the normal introduction and a man replies. Amy tells him to have a seat and then comes into the back room to tell us.

She steps through the curtain that divides the two rooms, a silly smile on her face and her hands gripped in front of her. "There's a Mr. Ferro here asking about pictures for his wedding. He said Sky is his fiancée's favorite photographer, and they want the biggest package we have. Better get out there, you two!"

~THE END~

COMING SOON:

SECRETS & LIES
A Ferro Family Serial

To ensure you don't miss the next
installment, text
AWESOMEBOOKS to 22828 and you will
get an email reminder on release day.

*****

THE ARRANGEMENT SERIES TV
Keep an eye out for THE
ARRANGEMENT series coming to life
this fall.

*****

MORE FERRO FAMILY BOOKS

BRYAN FERRO
~THE PROPOSITION~

*****

SEAN FERRO
~THE ARRANGEMENT~

******

PETER FERRO GRANZ
~DAMAGED~

******

JONATHAN FERRO
~STRIPPED~

Turn the page to read a free sample of
Jonathan Ferro's story.

STRIPPED

CHAPTER 1

CASSIE

Bruce claps his big beefy hands at us like we're misbehaving dogs. "Come on ladies! Hustle! The bachelor party isn't going to be much fun if we never get there. Damn, Gretchen, you aren't even dressed, yet?"

She laughs like he's funny, even though Bruce is as far from funny as a person could get. He's the bouncer at the club and on nights like tonight, he comes with us to keep the guys from getting handsy. Some rich brat out on Long Island rented us for the night. There are seven of us going to perform on stage, plus the stripping wait staff, and dear, sweet, Bruce.

Gretchen is piling her long golden hair onto the top of her head and securing it with a long bobby pin. She's strutting around half naked, as if we like looking at her. She smiles sweetly at Bruce and waves a hand, bending it at the wrist like he's silly. "Please, I'll be ready before Cassie even finishes lacing up her corset."

She tilts her head in my direction as I fumble with my corset hooks. Every time I manage to hook one, another comes undone. Whoever invented the corset should be burned at the stake. The stupid thing might look cool once it's on, but getting into it is a whole other matter. Add in the fact that mine is a real corset— meaning it has steel boning—and breathing isn't something I can do either. I got this thing because it was authentic. I thought that meant it had period fabric or grommets or something cool. It turns out that authentic means metal rods built into the bodice, guaranteed to bruise my ribs. Fuck, I hate this thing, but I refuse to throw it away—it cost me three weeks' pay at my old job. Plus, it's not like I wear it every night. We only pull out the good stuff on holidays and for special events like this.

Bruce turns his head my way and looks like he wants to pull out his hair. I'm nearly dressed, except for this contraption. My ensemble includes the candy apple colored corset, lace-topped thigh highs, and a delicate little G-string, coupled with heels that could be used as weapons. If I ever get mugged wearing these shoes, you can bet your ass that I won't run, not that I could. These are the things I think about when I make my purchases. Can this purse do some damage? Maybe I should skip the leather Dooney and grab me that metal no-name bag with the sharp corners. My roommate and I live across the street from a drug den. Don't even get me started on that. I know we need to move, but knowing it and affording it are two different things. In the meantime, I buy accessories that can be used as weapons.

Glaring at her, I reply, "Gee, thanks, Gretch." My fingers push the next bit of metal through the grommet. This one stays put.

She bats her glittering lashes at me. "No problem." Gretchen is tall and lanky with a larger-than-life super model thing going on. I hate her. She's a bitch with a capital B. It's all good, though. She hates me, too. It's difficult to be hostile toward someone that likes you. Gretchen makes it easy to hate her guts.

Me, I'm not a supermodel. I'm nothing to look at—my mom drilled that into my head a million times. I'm completely average with sub-par confidence, but I can act. I can fake it so that once I hit that stage, I'm as good as the rest of the strippers.

No, I didn't dream of being a pole dancer when I was a little kid, but my life took some wicked turns and here I am, dealing with it. There are worse things I suppose, although I won't be able to think of a single one when I'm letting a bunch of pervs rake their lusty eyes over my naked body. The truth is, I hate this. I'd rather be anywhere else, doing anything else. The gynecologist's office, sign me up. Root canal, no problem. I'll be there early and with a smile on my face. Anything is better than this.

Bruce lingers in the dressing room for too long, staring at his watch. His thick arms are folded over his broad chest as he watches the second hand tick off the passing time. He ignores Gretch's gibe at me. I may be newer, but I pull in a lot more cash and that's what the boss likes—lots of money. As long as I keep doing it, I have a job.

I finally get my corset hooked up when Beth walks by. She's already wearing some frilly satin thing. "Hey, Cassie. Do you want me to lace you up?"

Tucking a piece of hair behind my ear, I nod. "Yeah, thanks." She laces me in, pulling each X tightly, cinching me up until I can barely breathe. "Tight enough?"

I try to inhale deeply, and can't because the metal bars inside the fabric won't permit it. I nod and press my hands to the bodice, feeling the supple satin under my hands. "Yeah, tighter than that and I'll pass out—or pop a boob."

She laughs, "You're the only one who worries about stuff like that. You're so cute." She ties off the strings and tucks them in before swatting my back when she's finished. My boobs are hiked up so high that I can't see my toes when I look down. I grab my robe and wrap it around me as we head to the cars. It's going to be a long night.

———

The ride to the party is short. We're on the north shore of Long Island, not too far from the coast. There are tons of old homes with huge lawns and even bigger estate houses nestled out of sight between towering oaks and pines. The place hosting the party looks like a castle. We pass through the gates and drive around to the side of the house. The van stops and we're told the usual—go wait in the servants' wing until it's time.

Beth and I walk inside, shoulder to shoulder, whispering about the garish wealth that's practically dripping from the walls as we walk inside. Gretchen and a few other girls trail behind us, chattering about what kind of tips they'll make tonight. A party like this can line a girl's pockets for a month if it goes well, but for me it'll do more than that. You see, I'm the main event, the mystery girl in the pink room—the bachelor's private-party dancer. While my coworkers are off in the main hall, I'll be earning the big bucks. That's the main reason why Gretchen hates my guts. Before I came along, she was the top stripper around here.

It's getting late, which means the party is well under way. Beth picks up a tiny sandwich off a tray as she walks to the back of the bustling room. "You think this guy knows what's coming?"

I shrug. "Like it matters, anyway? When's the last time we were sent away?"

"Uh, never." She pops the food in her mouth and chews it up.

I'm leaning against a counter top with my elbows behind me, supporting my weight. "My point exactly. Guys are dicks. They commit to marrying a woman, but this kind of crap the night before the wedding is okay." I roll my eyes as I make a disgusted sound, and straighten up. All of a sudden I'm talking with my hands and they're flying all over the place, "Tell me, why would a guy want a lap dance if he's in love? You'd think he'd only want his bride, but that never happens. He's always happy to have an ass in his face."

"Well, your ass is pretty awesome, or so I've heard." Beth smirks at me and glances around the kitchen. We're in the way, but there isn't anywhere else for us to go yet.

"Guys suck, that's all I'm saying."

"I know. You've said it a million times." She makes a *roaring* sound and shakes her fist in the air before turning to me and grunting, "Men. Evil."

"You're an idiot." I smile at her, trying not to laugh.

She points at me and clicks her tongue. "Right back at you, Cassie."

Bruce waves us over to the other side of the kitchen. "Cassie, Beth—follow me." We duck out behind him and follow the guy down the hall and slip into a little room. It's been done up in pale pinks with silver curtains, similar to the room I work in at the club. Since this is a party, Bruce added another dancer and I got to choose. While I work the stage at the front of the room, Beth will work the floor.

Bruce points a beefy finger at the stage and says to us, "Take your places, and remember that this client is the shit. Pull out all the stops, say 'no' to nothing. You got it?"

We nod in unison. The stage is elevated off the floor, with a few steps up at either end. It looks like the stage is new, built just for me. People usually rent those gray, make-shift stages that wobble when walked on, but not this guy. They spared no expense. The walls are lined with pale pink silks and illuminated from the floor. Clear tables flicker around the room with pink flames dancing within. It's seductive. The colors blend together, reminding me of pale flesh and kissable pink lips. As I climb the steps up the side of the stage and head to the silvery tinsel curtain, I call back to Beth. "Who is this party for again? And why is he the shit? I must have missed the memo."

She laughs as she's examining one of the lights within the glass table. It looks like fire, but it can't be since it's pink. She looks up at me. "Dr. Peter Granz, and he's the shit because he's a Ferro. Hence the swank party." Beth looks up when I don't answer.

I rush at Beth, nearly knocking her over. My jaw is hanging open as worry darts across my face faster than I can contain it. "Ferro?"

"Yeah, why?"

I'm in melt down mode. "I can't be here." I glance around the room and look at the door longingly. Before I make up my mind to run, I hear male voices approaching. Fuck! My heart pounds faster in my chest. If he's here, if Jonathan sees me—the thought cuts off before it finishes.

I'm ready to bounce out the window when Beth grabs my wrist and hauls me to the front of the room. She shoves me behind the curtain and hisses in my ear, "If you freak out now, Gretchen will steal your job. Snap out of it. Whoever this guy is, he isn't worth it."

The tinsel curtain in front of me flutters, but it conceals both of us for the moment. The male voices grow louder until the door is yanked open. The curtain rustles and I'm in full freak-out mode. He can't be here. He can't see me like this. At the same time,

Beth's right. I can't skip out. Bruce will run me over with the van and there's no way in hell they'll ever give me another cent.

I stand there, frozen, unable to think. Every muscle in my body is strained, ready to run, but I don't move. My bare feet remain glued to the floor as I smash my lips together.

Then, I hear it—that voice. It floats through the air like a familiar old song. Oh God, someone shoot me. I can't do this. "You don't know what you're talking about. What guy wouldn't want a party like this?" Jonathan is talking to someone in that light, charming, tone of his.

"Uh, your brother, Peter. Do you know the guy at all? He's going to act like he loves it and get the hell out before you can blink." Glancing through the curtains, I can see the second man. He has dark hair and bright blue eyes like Jonathan. The only difference is their posture. Jonathan has all his weight thrown onto one hip with his arms folded across his chest. The other guy's spine is ramrod straight, like he's never slouched in his life.

Peering at Jonathan through the tinsel, I see a perfect smile lace his lips. "Sean, I know him better than that. Pete is going to love this. It's exactly the kind of party I'd want if I was getting hitched."

"Yes, I know." Sean's voice is flat. He glances around the room with disgust, and slips his hands into his pockets. "Don't say I didn't warn you."

"Oh come on! It's Peter. What's he going to do?"

Sean laughs, like he knows something that Jonathan doesn't. "Don't let that English teacher façade fool you, Jonny. He's as hot headed as I am. No one fucks with him. He's going to consider this a slap in the face, an insult to Sidney. Cancel the strippers before he gets here." Sean leaves the room without another word.

Jonathan Ferro lets out a rush of air and runs his fingers through his thick, dark, hair. The aggravated sound that comes out of his mouth kills me. I've heard it before, I know him too well to not be affected by it. That's the sound he makes when he knows he's screwed up, when he sees that he isn't the man he wants to be. There's always been this wall between Jonathan and his family. I guess he still hasn't gotten past it. Jon paces in a circle a few times and then darts out of the room.

"Holy shit." Beth looks at me and hisses, "What happened between you and him?"

It feels like icy fingers have wrapped around my heart and squeezed. I stare after him and utter, "Nothing, absolutely nothing."

CHAPTER 2

JONATHAN

Why does everyone think they know my brothers better than I do? I'm taking advice from Sean. How the hell did that happen? I'm walking swiftly down the long hallway, chin tucked, not watching where I'm going. The golden wallpaper appears to be glowing in the dim light. I run my hands through my hair and down my neck, and smack into someone.

When I look up, I'm ready to snap. "What the— Oh, it's you."

My closest friend, Trystan Scott, is standing in front of me. The guy is the brother I never had. He's not blood, but he might as well be called a Ferro because he's that loyal.

Trystan's wearing ripped jeans, a button down shirt with the top three buttons undone, and has way too much shit in his hair. "What the hell's going on? I thought the waitresses were supposed to be strippers. That was the coolest idea you've ever had. Imagine my disappointment when I rush out of rehearsal—away from the sexiest woman you've ever seen—and get here to find a bunch of chicks still wearing clothes." Trystan smirks and shoves his hands in his pockets.

I don't bother to answer him before resuming full speed down the hall. I have to find the guy from the club and cancel my awesome plan. Damn it, why does Peter have to be so difficult. Who doesn't want strippers at a bachelor party?

Trystan follows behind. "So, how's it going?" His voice has that teasing tone, which means he knows how well it's going.

"Nice hair," I throw back, and glance at him out of the corner of my eyes. Trystan makes a face and tries to smooth it down, but it doesn't move. "What'd they use, glue?"

His dark hair is sticking up all over the place. It looks like a porcupine toupee. "Something like that. I look like a fucking idiot."

"Yeah, but it's not the hair that does it—it's the make-up."

"Awh, fuck." Trystan swipes his hand across his eyes, trying to rub it off. "I forgot. I had somewhere to be—somewhere with strippers—so I ran over here as fast as I could." He smacks my arm with the back of his hand. "So, come on Jon, what's going on?"

"Apparently this isn't Pete's MO. I'm canceling the girls before Peter gets here. Sean said he'd bolt, that titties aren't his thing."

"Titties are his thing, but he prefers a certain pair." Trystan grins and looks over at me, pressing his hand to his chest. "The ways of the heart are—"

"And what would you know about that? You're a goddamn legend. You've nailed every chick from coast to coast."

Trystan's smile brightens, but it's like there's something he's not telling me. Ever since I met him a few years ago, he's been like that. He doesn't talk about his past much, but I don't blame him. From the papers, I know Trystan's dad beat the shit out of him when he was a kid, but that's about it. The guy keeps to himself, but somehow manages to get pussy whenever he wants. A shy rock star is a fucking oxymoron, but the women fall at his feet. What do I know? Maybe I've been doing everything wrong this whole time. I shake the thoughts away and enter the main room.

The music pounds through the air, vibrating through me. The dim lights make it difficult to see the guy I'm looking for. He should be back in the kitchen right about now. I lean into Trystan. "I'll catch you later."

"Whatever you need, man." Trystan grabs my arm and squeezes. He's saying he's got my back, even if no one else does. The guy might be a train wreck, but he's good people under all that shit.

I slap his back, "Thanks. Catch you in a few. We can hit the bar after Pete gets here, because I'm not walking around sober if there's only guys here." Trystan laughs and agrees to get smashed with me later. You got to love the guy.

I weave through the crowd. There are already some strippers posing as wait staff. A woman with a tray and way too much make-up on her face brushes my side and turns toward me. "Champagne?" Her cleavage is up to her neck and the thin white shirt she's wearing does nothing to hide the black bra underneath. Fuck, she's hot. I almost stop and flirt with her—almost—but I keep walking, because I'm not a total dick. This was supposed to be for Pete. I need to fix this before he gets here.

Sean falls in step beside me. "Tell me that I didn't see Scott at the bar?" Sean hates anyone who wasn't born with the name Ferro.

"Fuck off, Sean. He's my friend."

"He's using you." Sean's jaw is locked tight as he scans the crowd. "You're too naïve."

"You're an asshole." I'm not defending my friendship with Trystan or with anyone else. Sean acts like he knows everything, and he might be right most of the time, but he's wrong about Trystan. "The guy has his own millions. He doesn't need mine."

"He's unstable."

"You're unstable." I flick my eyes over to him.

Sean smirks. "Possibly."

"I can't chat about your mental health right now. I need to find the guy before all these girls rip their clothes off. Where's Pete?"

Sean laughs and points across the room. "He just got here."

"Fuck." I take off through the crowd, cutting through the guys, shoving some aside.

When I push through the kitchen doors, I see him. "Bruce! My man—change of plans."

Bruce is a huge guy and doesn't look pleased to see me. There are half dressed girls everywhere, slipping into their tear off waitressing outfits. Damn, this would have been so cool. Bruce has his thigh-thick arms folded over his chest. He glares at me. "No refunds."

"I'm not asking for one." I stand in front of the guy and feel like a toothpick, even though I'm not. Reaching into my pocket, I feel around for a hundred dollar bill. "I need them to keep their clothes *on*."

He gives me a weird look. "They're not supposed to be waitresses, Mr. Ferro. They're strippers and are expecting the tips that accompany the occupation."

Okay, I grab a fist full of bills and slip them into his hand. Bruce takes it and sees how much I've given him. I ask, "Maybe they could be waitresses for a couple of hours and then head out?"

"Maybe, but this isn't going to help the girls you hired for the private room. They're expecting tips, and if you cancel them out, they'll have left the club for nothing. You have to make good over there." The guy's voice is dangerously deep.

"Done. I'll go take care of it." I reach out and shake his hand.

As I turn to leave he clears his throat. "And if you'd like this kept quiet…"

I reach into my pocket and slap more cash into his fist. Bastard. The large man grins. "My lips are sealed, Mr. Ferro. A suggestion?" he asks, and I nod as my gaze cuts across the room to the clock. "Keep at least one girl in that private room for your guests. This is a party that people will talk about. You don't want them to think you're a pussy. You've got a reputation that people know about. They expect a little something extra at one of your parties."

"And you know this because…?"

"Because I've got ears, Mr. Ferro. Every man here is wondering what your big surprise will be this evening. You need to keep something for them, don't you?"

I don't answer him, because I know he's right. "Fine, I'll go speak to them. You keep the girls out here clothed."

Bruce laughs and leans back in his chair. "Done."

When I get back to the private room, I push through the doors without really paying attention until I hear a voice—that voice. It's like being hit in the face with a wall of cold water. Whatever thought I had in my head is gone. Wide eyed, I look up and scan the room. Two women are tangled together on the floor, fighting. Well, no they're not fighting, not really. I'm not sure what they're doing, and they have no idea I'm watching.

My heart pounds harder as her voice fills my head and I try to see her face. My body responds the way it used to—that hollow spot in the center of my chest aches, along with my cock. I stare in disbelief, watching two strippers wrestling on the floor, and stand in shock because one of them is Cassie Hale.

STRIPPED IS AVAILABLE NOW

MORE ROMANCE BOOKS BY

H.M. WARD

DAMAGED

DAMAGED 2

STRIPPED

SCANDALOUS

SCANDALOUS 2

SECRETS

THE SECRET LIFE OF
TRYSTAN SCOTT

And more.

To see a full book list, please visit:
www.SexyAwesomeBooks.com

CAN'T WAIT FOR H.M WARD'S NEXT STEAMY BOOK?

☆☆☆☆☆

Let her know by leaving stars and telling
her what you liked about
THE WEDDING CONTRACT
in a review!